Get the hell out of town...

"...I want you lost to human ken until I can do something about that senator and his hired gun crew, dammit. So far, you've only managed to gun *one* of Senator Winger's so-called bodyguards, and Lord preserve us all if you wind up shooting the senator himself!"

"Is he really that hot-tempered?" Longarm asked mildly.

Vail replied soberly, "He is. Why did you think he always travels with a pack of bodyguards? In his salad days he fancied himself Colorado's answer to James Butler Hickok, and right now he's gunning for you, personal. So, like I said, get lost from human ken. I don't want to see you myself until you bring in that prisoner sometime next week. And if you mess up on *that* chore, I never want to see you again, hear?"

TABOR EVANS

LONGARM

AND THE
TREACHEROUS TRIAL

J

JOVE BOOKS, NEW YORK

LONGARM AND THE TREACHEROUS TRIAL

A Jove Book/published by arrangement with
the author

PRINTING HISTORY
Jove edition/September 1988

All rights reserved.
Copyright © 1988 by Jove Publications, Inc.
This book may not be reproduced in whole or in part,
by mimeograph or any other means, without permission.
For information address: The Berkley Publishing Group,
200 Madison Avenue, New York, New York 10016.

ISBN: 0-515-09707-1

Jove Books are published by The Berkley Publishing Group,
200 Madison Avenue, New York, New York 10016.
The name "JOVE" and the "J" logo
are trademarks belonging to Jove Publications, Inc.

PRINTED IN THE UNITED STATES OF AMERICA

10 9 8 7 6 5 4 3 2 1

Chapter 1

Longarm had long since learned there were times for deep thinking and there were times for fast action. So as the gunsmoke commenced to clear, his first conscious thought about the two shots he'd just fired was a sober consideration of how close his quick-draw contest with a total stranger had just been.

Then, the tall deputy proceeded to reload his double-action .44-40 as he morosely regarded the loser at his feet in the adobe dust of a downtown Denver alleyway. The stranger lay faceup with two sticky red roses of blood pinned to the frilly white shirtfront he'd donned ahead of his darker red vest and black frock coat. His pearl-gray Stetson now hung neatly from a climbing spike driven into a nearby telegraph pole. One dead hand still held the nickel-plated Harrington & Richardson over the fly of his gray pants, as if it were a fig leaf and he didn't want the world to notice how he'd pissed his britches on his way to Hell.

Longarm heard the not-too-distant twittering of a police whistle and lowered his own gun politely to his side. Such tweets were only to be expected when one shot it out in an alley smack between the city hall and county courthouse, even in a town of more modest dimensions than Denver.

The first blue uniform on the scene encased the husky form of Sergeant Nolan, Denver P.D. So Longarm felt it safe to put his still-warm but reloaded weapon back in the cross-draw holster he packed it in, under the tobacco-tweed frock coat his own job called for, at least in town, since the somewhat sissy Hayes administration had cracked down on the old rough-and-ready ways of the Justice Department.

But Longarm learned how little pull he really had with the Denver P.D. when Sergeant Nolan asked, cheerfully enough, who he might have shot this time, and how come.

Longarm said soberly, "I'm still working on that part. I was on my way to work as usual, cutting through this alley to save a few steps and avoid some of the morning rush, when I encountered this gent striding the other way. The results you see before you."

Nolan waved back another couple of copper badges responding to the dulcet sounds of firearms discharged within the city limits, then turned back to Longarm to say softly, "Dammit, old pard, you got to do better than that. I know you're a deputy federal marshal, and I can see that piss-soaked whore-pistol the dead man seems to be holding so modest. But, Jesus H. Christ, this here is the capital of Colorado, with streetcars running along both Broadway and Colfax, and it ain't been called Cherry Creek Camp for some time. You may find this hard to grasp, Longarm, but there's a city ordinance against shooting at *lampposts* in this town. Who ever told you it was lawful to shoot at human beings on my beat?"

Longarm reached under his coat, hauled out a couple of three-for-a-nickel cheroots, and handed one to Nolan as he answered simply, "He did. The moment we locked eyes I saw it was him or me. You forgot the new opera house, by the way, but no town could be sissy enough to deny a taxpaying resident the right of self-defense."

Nolan struck a light for both of them as he pointed out, "The day you pay city taxes on them hired digs of yours on the far side of the creek will be the day our precinct-house cat starts putting out for the mice. But let's stick to the reality of this gent you just shot, twice, just above the heart. Which one of you drew first?"

Longarm blew a smoke ring toward the sprawled remains at their feet and replied, "I did, of course. Can't you see the patent evidence of your own eyes? It's a simple fact of nature that the one who gets his gun out first is usually the winner."

"Dammit, Longarm," Nolan protested, "there's no argument about who *won* here. You got to do better with how come you slapped leather on the poor cuss to begin with!"

Longarm shrugged and insisted, "I had to. We met. We locked eyes. It's hard to explain in words, but by the time you've worn a gun as long as me, if you're still alive, you just know when it's time to go for it. So I did and, as you can see, he *still* got his out on the way down, knowing he was dead."

The older but less-experienced lawman, Nolan, sighed and said, "Look, Longarm, I know you of old, and if it was up to me alone, I would feel inclined to buy your explanation, carefree as I have to say it sounds. But it ain't up to me and it's going to appear even dumber on paper. You can't excuse this infernal mess by just allowing you didn't cotton to the looks of a

3

total stranger and so you figured you ought to gun him, right behind the city hall!"

Longarm tried, "He went for his own gun as well, right?"

But Nolan shook his head and said, "Self-defense works both ways. What a man might or might not do after he'd been hit twice at close range is neither here nor there."

But that gave Nolan a grand notion. So he dropped to one knee by the cadaver, disarmed the dead man's hand, and sniffed at the Harrington & Richardson hopefully. Then he grimaced and said, "Gun oil and piss. Ain't been fired since it was cleaned. Let me see if there's any I.D. to go with his innocent side arm."

There was. Nolan found an expensive pigskin billfold in an inside pocket of the expensive frock coat, opened it, and let out a low, mournful whistle before he told Longarm, "It appears you just ended the career of one John Henry Calhoun, licensed by this very state of Colorado as a private detective."

Longarm grimaced and said, "That could explain the murderous look of recognition I met up with in his eyes. The name's a fake, if I had cause to remember it from some past events. But a lot of bounty hunters take the trouble of buying themselves such a license before they gun anybody. For one thing, it can save them tedious conversations like the one *we* seem to be having."

Longarm took a thoughtful drag on his cheroot before he went on. "My own views on bounty hunters are well known. Knowing I might take considerable interest in anyone who killed for hire in these parts, and seeing he had me alone back here, with neither witnesses nor apparent suspicions of his disgusting habits on my part, he likely figured he'd never have a better chance, so—"

"He figured wrong," Nolan cut in, getting back to his

4

feet and dusting off a blue-serge knee as he continued, "We'll run the name and license number through our files for you. There's an outside chance the state issued a hunting license to a wanted man. It happens. Meanwhile, we'd best go on over to the precinct house and see if the captain will let us cut you loose of your own recognizance, for now."

"Are you saying I'm under arrest?" asked Longarm quietly.

Nolan gulped but proved he rated his stripes by saying, "I am. I know we're pals, Longarm, but you did just kill a man on my beat, for no sensible reason *I* can fully grasp."

The precinct captain was another old pal, but nevertheless it was pushing noon by the time Longarm finally got to work that morning. As he strode into the U.S. Marshal's office on the second floor of the Denver Federal Building, the young squirt who played the typewriter out front shot Longarm a snide look and asked if he knew what time it was.

Longarm nodded soberly and replied, "Going on eleven forty-five, Henry. Don't push it. I'd have gotten here sooner if I hadn't had to gun *another* wiseass whose middle name was Henry."

Then he strode on into the inner sanctum of Marshal William Vail, Denver District Court, to see how much trouble he was in. Unlike old Henry out front, Longarm's boss got to sass him some.

But, though braced for a chewing, Longarm made it to the big leather chair across the cluttered desk from old Billy Vail without suffering the usual sarcasm. The older, shorter, and fatter Vail did cast a wistful glance at the banjo clock on one oak-paneled wall. But he looked more sympathetic than angry as he lit one of his own big

5

black cigars, shook out the match, and growled, "I heard. I can square your morning workout with the Denver D.A. After that it gets more complicated. The late Johnny Reb Calhoun had a well-established rep as a trigger-happy son of a bitch with everything from chicken theft to murder-in-the-first on his yellow sheets. But they let him out of Yuma Prison six months ago with his many debts to society paid in full."

Longarm lit a less-expensive as well as less-stinky smoke in self-defense before he replied, "I reckon he was out to run his account with the law up some more, then. One look into them mad-dog eyes would have convinced even old Henry, out front, it was time to draw or die. I did what I had to. I'm glad the Denver D.A. is such a sensible cuss, though."

Vail shrugged and asked, "What are friends for?" Then he had to spoil it all by adding, "None of the local lawmen I drink with at all regular are the problem, old son. The problem is that the rascal you shot it out with was the personal bodyguard of Senator Howard Winger. They say his yard dog's part wolf as well. Need we say more?"

Longarm flicked some tobacco ash on the rug in case any carpet beetles were down there plotting mischief and told Vail, "We surely do, boss. I never shot it out with nobody guarding any fool senator. He came at me solo, with death in his eyes and a whore-pistol in his shoulder rig."

Vail nodded but said, "You never should have told the local law you beat him to the draw. Like you said, there was nary one witness. You should have said he drew first, you idiot."

Longarm shrugged, fed the carpet beetles some more ash, and said, "You raised me as an honest lawman, and it's against the law to swear out a false deposition. If there had been witness-one, he or she might have been proud to swear both our hands were in sort of sudden motion at the same time. It was as fair a fight as such fights ever go, Billy. Naturally the winner always has some edge. That's how one gets to be the winner, see?"

Billy Vail said, "I see, and the D.A. sees, but Senator Winger says he can't, and he's mad as hell at the rest of us. So stop dumping ashes on my infernal carpet and listen tight."

Longarm put the cheroot back between his teeth as Vail rummaged through the papers on his desk, muttering, "Lord save us all from cowboy superstitions. Tobacco ash ain't good for carpets and it just ain't true that cowshit is good for bullet wounds, either. Here we go."

Longarm took the rumpled sheet of onionskin paper the older lawman thrust his way across the desk. But Vail said, "Don't try to read nothing but the names and addresses near the top. I keep telling Henry not to use carbon paper more than thrice but he's superstitious too. I can tell you about the mission faster than even I could read it. I'm sending you over to the town of Stateline, on the Ogallala Trail, to pick up and transport a federal prisoner. Are you with me so far?"

Longarm just had to flick ash some damned place. So he took off his dark Stetson and made sure no moths were lurking in the inside creases of his Colorado crush as he replied, "Sure. I can see why you'd want to send a deputy with my seniority on a fool's errand, seeing as that fool senator is so upset about losing his pet killer. How long do you want me to take getting yonder and back, boss? We're only talking a hundred miles and change, going and coming."

Billy Vail shot him a thoughtful look, then said, "I might've known you made friends with some fool female the last time I sent you over that way. But, right,

7

we want to give old Winger a chance to cool down or maybe get mad at someone else. So let's say you bill us six cents a mile going and twelve cents a mile coming back with the want and, oh, the rest of this week at a dollar per diem and no more. If you can manage a honeymoon suite at single rates I can take a joke as good as the next man. But no more bullshit about having to board a material witness just to witness her with her duds off, hear?"

Longarm smiled sheepishly and said, "They don't have any fancy hotels in that bitty trail town, Billy. They'd just finished mushrooming Stateline out of raw lumber the last time I passed that way. Let's see, now. If I get there Friday, on a sort of slow train, sleep late on Saturday and then, respecting the Sabbath, pick up my prisoner on Monday for a sort of slow ride back—"

"Pick him up Monday or Tuesday and make the trip back sudden with him in irons," Vail cut in, adding, "I mean that. Waste all the time you want *before* you take Big Bob Bacon off their hands. But once you've got him, don't shilly-shally. He's not the sort of owlhoot I want even a senior deputy taking chances with, see?"

Longarm frowned thoughtfully and said, "Not hardly. I pride my fool self for remembering dangerous wants and, to tell the truth, I never heard of this old boy before. I recall some discussion regarding a Nasty *Nate* Bacon and his gang, but—"

"Same outfit," Vail cut in. "Big Bob is Nasty Nate's little brother. To date he's failed to become as famous because they've generally let him hold the horses whilst Nasty Nate and the bigger boys go in to rob the whatever. But one of the things the gang robbed, recent, was the finance office at Fort Collins, making it Federal."

Vail took a drag on his own stinky smoke and then, since rank had its privileges, dropped the ashes on the rug on his side of the desk before continuing. "Keeping bad company can get even a lad just holding horses in trouble. So when the law in Stateline noticed Big Bob coming out of a house of ill repute they grabbed him, even though neither the rest of the gang nor their horses was in sight. They're holding him for us in the town lockup, even though he keeps insisting his name is John Smith."

Longarm shrugged and opined, "He don't sound so dangerous."

"He may not be," Vail replied, "although they do say he's even bigger than you are. The reason I want you to bring him in fast and alive, and I mean that about *alive*, is that his gang may try to rescue him or, failing that, kill him. Nasty Nate and the other members of the gang *are* dangerous!"

Longarm said, "I can see why they call the leader nasty if he figures to kill his own kid brother, for Pete's sake."

Vail nodded and said, "Nate's nasty, all right. But the main reason he might have for killing kin goes with Big Bob being sort of stupid as well as big. They know as well as we know that once we have Big Bob in federal custody, facing a few short years in Leavenworth, making army shoes, or a rope dance if he chooses to tough it out with us—"

"What could even a talkative prisoner tell us that we don't already know?" Longarm cut in.

Vail scowled, told him not to butt into adult conversations, and explained, "We know the names of everyone in the Bacon gang, and if they've done anything we don't know about, we still got enough to hang 'em in a bunch. What we don't have even an educated guess about is where in thunder they've managed to hide out so good between jobs. Federal, state, and territorial posses have hunted high and low for such a famous bunch, for some time, to no avail. It's our fervent hope that Big Bob may see fit to inform us of the gang's current address. So, while I can go along with your notions of rough justice, within reason, you'd best have one hell of a good reason for not bringing in this particular want alive and well, or well enough to *talk*, at least."

Longarm folded the flimsy excuse old Henry had typed up for him and put it away in the unlikely event anyone was ever going to want to read it. He knew the town law in Stateline and, so far, seemed on good enough terms with 'em. He rose to his considerable height and told Vail, "I see small need to fetch my old saddle and such from home. My landlady will likely want me to eat one of her awful boardinghouse spreads, and I'm sure they'll have a seat for me somewhere on the trains I'll be riding, anyway. So I reckon I'd best mosey over to the Parthenon and kill some time before the evening eastbound pulls out."

Vail shook his bullet head and snapped, "Don't you dare show your fool face in the Parthenon Saloon, and that goes for the Black Cat and Pronghorn while I'm at it. I want you lost to human ken until I can do something about that senator and his hired gun crew, dammit. So far, you've only managed to gun *one* of Senator Winger's so-called bodyguards, and Lord preserve us all if you wind up shooting the senator himself!"

"Is he really that hot-tempered?" Longarm asked mildly.

Vail replied soberly, "He is. Why did you think he always travels with a pack of bodyguards? In his salad days he fancied himself Colorado's answer to James Butler Hickok, and right now he's gunning for you, personal. So, like I said, get lost from human ken. I don't want to see you myself until you bring in that prisoner sometime next week. And if you mess up on *that* chore, I never want to see you again, hear?"

Longarm nodded and left, holding his overturned hat like the big ashtray he'd made of it, and feeling a mite foolish about it.

Out in the marble corridor, he turned the Stetson over to beat the ashes out of it. As he did so another door down the hall opened and the buxom little blonde stenographer popping out at him looked sort of confused by his odd actions. So he nodded at her pleasantly and said, "Marble mites. Tobacco ash is the best thing for marble mites, you know."

She didn't look at all convinced. But she didn't actually call for help as he put the hat back on, ticked the brim of it to her, and headed for the stairwell.

Less than an hour later, up on Sherman Avenue, another buxom blonde stared even more wild-eyed at Longarm when she opened her front door to see him standing there with a bunch of sunflowers he'd picked for her on the capitol grounds just down the way.

"Custis Long," she said, "I've always known you were loco en la cabeza. But what gives you the right to think I was out of my own poor head as well?"

He smiled down at her in a way that made her knees go weak under the thin shantung housedress she'd slipped into to answer the door. He said, "I know you told me never to darken your door again, little darling. You were right as rain when you said I had no right to drop by unexpected and sort of infrequent, but—"

"Don't try to sweet-talk me," she cut in. "A poor old widow woman has to expect to be treated as a port in the storm by such a handsome son of a bitch. But enough is goddammit enough! I forgave you for that redhead at the Black Cat, seeing as you were drunk and

11

all. But if you think I'm about to share you with that damned Chinese waitress at the Golden Dragon, you got another thing coming! How could you have done such a disgusting thing, you sex-mad moose? Don't you know half them Chinese have leprosy or worse?"

He grinned sheepishly and said, "I can't think of nothing worse than leprosy. But I ain't got it. I'll be proud to show you, once we're out of these stuffy duds."

She gulped weakly and suggested, "The least you could offer would be a heated denial of the gossip about you and that slant-eyed hussy, dammit."

He shook his head and said, "I never listen to gossip. What would you like to bet the same old biddy hens who gossip about innocent china dolls gossip just as disgusting about a sweet young thing like you?"

She gasped, shot an anxious look past him at the window curtains across the way and almost sobbed, "Oh, Lord, you're giving me the name without the game, standing there with those flowers and not a chaperone between us! Please go away, Custis. My mind is made up, this time, and surely that head matron at the orphan asylum can't be mad at you as well right now?"

That was the trouble with gossip. Most of the damned time it was accurate. So Miss Morgana Floyd of the Arvada Orphan Asylum had heard about his fling with the Oriental waitress as well. But as he shrugged and started to turn away, he tried, "Well, seeing all my old pals have turned against me, I'll just have to make my stand alone, maybe over on the Capitol grounds. I might have a chance if they have to charge uphill at me under fire."

As Longarm had hoped, whether she was really sore at him or not, no member of the female species could resist demanding a further explanation of *that*. So he said, "It's just a personal misunderstanding between me and a gang of hired guns. I'll likely make it through the night, Lord willing and the creeks don't rise. I've already beat one of 'em to the draw, so far."

"Oh, Custis!" she gasped. "You're in trouble, I mean in *real* trouble, and you're standing there with your back exposed to the street? Come inside this instant, you big goof! For nobody but me has the right to harm a hair on your cheating head, you bastard!"

Never having had a crack at Queen Victoria herself, Longarm would never be able to make up his mind, for sure, whether it was the Widow of Windsor or all the ladies who considered it so high-toned to imitate her, but *somebody* was surely working overtime at impractical purity. He did know, from personal experience, how many late-Victorian women managed to cope with current social standards and the simple facts of nature at the same time without resorting to suicide or strong drugs. It would have been called hypocrisy if any Victorian who took it serious to act like a Victorian ever admitted to a single vice. But, since they never, more pragmatic men of their world, like Longarm, had to either catch them at it or assume in a good-natured way that it really didn't matter how much masturbation or slap-and-tickle with the servants went on behind closed doors.

Getting the front door of the widow's house on Sherman Avenue closed behind him was half the battle. The rest of the battle took a mite longer but followed a predictable course. He'd have never attacked this particular stronghold of respectability with only an afternoon to kill if he hadn't had more than one tactical advantage to begin with.

As he'd known before picking sunflowers for her, the junoesque young widow living lonesome in the big old brownstone her husband had left her on Capitol Hill had no live-in help, not because she couldn't afford them, but because she valued her privacy more than she hated picking up after herself. That was what she called her habit of wandering about the premises bare-assed in high summer: privacy. Not even Queen Victoria could expect a pleasantly plump young lady to stay gussied up in whalebone stays and itchy duds from sweaty throat to fashionably cramped toes *all* the time and, when she wasn't lounging about her house in bare-assed privacy, the young woman spent a heap of time at the opera, charity balls, and such.

The second unfair advantage her chosen lifestyle gave a man with the sense to notice was that, unlike eight out of ten of her high-toned neighbors along Sherman Avenue, the pretty young widow didn't like to drink alone and knew the patent medicines a lot of her teetotal neighbors took for their "female complaints" were at least a hundred proof, with or without opium added. Hence it was a safe bet that should she decide to receive a visitor at all, he'd find her not only close to bare-assed but able and willing to function as a healthy young woman of some experience.

The third advantage Longarm had over her, and she protested it was simply unfair, was that he'd already laid her on previous visits. So after he laid her some more she grudgingly decided to forgive him, just this one more time, if he'd let her get on top.

But later, as they lay sprawled across her rumpled sheets upstairs, sharing a smoke as the sunset light through her lace curtains etched interesting patterns on their naked flesh, she naturally reverted, as all women tend to, once they've had their wicked way with a gent, from a wanton goddess of love to an inquisitive female. So she made Longarm tell her the whole story and,

14

once he had, she wrinkled her pert nose and decided, "Pooh, you just took poor old Windy Winger's threats at face value as an excuse to get back in my good graces again, bless your ingenious soul. You knew those weedy flowers never would have done it, even with chocolate thrown in."

He patted her firm if somewhat heroic rump fondly with the free hand he had down her back and told her, "You warned me never to bring you any more chocolate, remember? I don't know why, but it's your figure. As for taking the threats of a senator who runs in packs serious, I could sure use some words of cheer on *that* subject, honey. Do you *know* the cuss?"

She snuggled closer and enjoyed a drag on his cheroot before she placed it back in Longarm's face, saying, "I know his wife, Regina, better. She grew up here in Denver, albeit I have to say she was born somewhere else and arrived by covered wagon with the rest of us about the time of the Cherry Creek strike."

Longarm mused, "That would have been back in the late fifties, making her somewhere on the fibbing side of thirty if she wasn't born out here with the rest of you sweet young things, right?"

The sweet young thing he was in bed with sniffed and said, *"My* age is none of your damned business, you brute. Regina Winger must be closer to forty, albeit well preserved and, I have to say it, nice enough, considering her background."

Longarm cocked an eyebrow to ask, "Oh? Are you saying she's as spiteful as her man, the senator, or are we gossiping about her table manners and such?"

"I'm sure she smokes in bed," she said. "But she's all right, I guess. Nobody has a temper like Windy Winger. He's older than she is, say somewhere in his fifties, and nobody who grew up in Denver, even on your side of Cherry Creek, could have such awful manners. He's one of those self-made mining moguls, like Leadville Johnny Brown or poor pompous Silver Dollar Tabor, only *they,* at least, *tried* to learn to eat with knife and fork once they hit pay dirt. Windy Winger sort of glories in his hardscrabble days as a prospector and, some say, a claim jumper. I don't know how poor Regina puts up with him or, for that matter, how much of it is just an act. You men out here are so silly about electing men your wives would never allow you to bring home for supper."

Longarm chuckled and said, "I never voted for the ruffian, and it's a good thing for us that I don't have to worry about who a wife might want me associating with." Then he brightened and said, "Hold on. Seeing as you *do* get on better with the senator's wife than I get along with the senator..."

But she shook her somewhat disheveled blonde head to tell him to forget it, explaining, "I only know her well enough to howdy, not well enough to ask her to ask her husband to leave my lover alone. Like I said, she was older than me, growing up, and, well, to tell the truth, her folk were considered trash by my folk and I wouldn't have been allowed to associate with her if we *had* been closer in age and address."

Then she began to fondle him soothingly as she added, "Your boss, that otherwise ornery old Billy Vail, may have come up with the best way to deal with Windy Winger, dearheart. Since the old fool got himself elected a few years back, he and poor Regina get to spend most of their time back east, in Washington. They're just out here because of the elections coming up this fall and, as Billy Vail says, the mean-tempered fool has a lot of other worries on his feeble mind. I don't see how he can hope to carry on a blood feud and get re-elected at the same time, do you?"

Longarm grimaced and said, "Gents rich enough to hire private armies don't have to feud, personal. I wonder why in thunder old Senator Winger feels he *needs* all them hired guns around him. It ain't like an Indian uprising seems likely in the District of Columbia, or even here in Denver."

"Well," she said, "he does campaign a lot in places like Creede and Durango, dear. Few folk who can read without moving their lips would ever vote for him. He campaigns as a sort of rough-talking hardrock man with leftist labor notions when he's orating at the total illiterates, or a free-silver and low-wages platform when he's in a smoke-filled room with his richer backers. I know I, for one, would like to see him assassinated or at least out of office. Maybe that's what he's worried about."

Longarm reached his free arm out to get rid of the almost shot cheroot as he sighed and said, "I'm sure glad I never voted for him. But I sure hope you and old Billy are right about him cooling off as sudden as he heats up. For the elections aren't 'til November, and I can't hide out from the fool and his hired guns *that* long!"

She asked him if he wanted to bet, as she rolled over and began to kiss her way down his naked belly toward the prize she had gripped in one hand, almost painfully tight. As he grasped her intent he chuckled and said, "Well, like I said downstairs before we got to be pals again, I'm under direct orders to take a lot of time getting over to Stateline. But it's a good thing for you I'm only a *federal* lawman. I believe I've told you more than once that blowing the French horn is a statute offense in this here state of Colorado."

She rolled onto her knees and allowed her unbound

blonde hair to cascade into his lap as she studied the object of her desire in an almost clinical way and told it, "Well, you don't *look* like you suffer from leprosy, you poor sweet thing. But Lord knows where that naughty Custis has been shoving you, or how else he's been abusing you."

Longarm growled through gritted teeth, "Speaking of abuse, I sure wish you'd quit abusing it or kiss it and make it well!"

She giggled, teased him yet more cruelly with the tip of her darting tongue, and said, "Hmmm, I don't *taste* any soy sauce, but I don't know, Custis. Just thinking about this poor thing, hard as this, anywhere near the privates of a heathen Chinese . . ."

"Goddammit," he said, "you have my word that anything you may have heard about me and any pagan ladies in or about the Golden Dragon is a pure fabrication of some mean-hearted white gal who'd no doubt be treating me nicer, right now, if I'd let her!"

The teasing white lady, who'd been upset by the gossip even more than she'd let on, gave a happy little sigh and asked him soberly, "Do you mean that, Custis? Do I really have your word?" And, when he assured her she goddammit did, she gave a happy cry of womankind triumphant and proceeded to swallow him alive.

He liked it. Any man would have. But, like any other man in such interesting surroundings, Longarm preferred not to even wonder where, or with whom, such a high-toned society gal might have learned to take it deeper down her throat than many a gal who did it for a living was willing to. So, having been aroused to full attention in a manner disapproved by most state statutes, Longarm rolled her on her back, spread-eagle, to finish in her in the manner approved of by Queen Victoria, albeit it seemed doubtful old Prince Albert had ever pounded quite as hard or deep. He'd been a sort of puny gent who'd died young. That was maybe one of the reasons late-Victorian moral codes had wound up so confused.

When they'd finished, for the moment, to lie weak and friendly in a pile of still-quivering flesh, the buxom blonde under Longarm murmured, "Oh, that was so lovely, dear. I wasn't really able to let myself go all the way until you assured me the gossip about you and that heathen Chinese was a lie. Why do you suppose anyone would start such a vicious story, dearheart?"

He said he didn't know. That was true, when one studied on it, for he had no idea who'd spotted him slipping in and out of that Chinese gal's quarters. He knew he hadn't lied, exactly, when he denied having anything to do with a heathen Chinese, because the pretty little thing had assured him, personal, that her folk had been converted by Christian missionaries.

Chapter 2

And so, the following afternoon, having slept the sleep of the just part of the time, and now walking a mite funny because of the rest of the time, Longarm left town discreetly aboard an eastbound combination of the Kansas & Pacific Line. Said line was sort of bragging about running from Kansas City to the Pacific, since it sort of petered out at the Denver Union Depot. But it still beat walking. The freight cars were up front; the coaches and club car were naturally aft. Longarm waited until they were rolling across open prairie without incident before he ambled back to the club car. He thoughtfully sized up the crowd back there from the doorway before entering. He saw nobody there who matched any Wanted fliers or recent prison releases. He knew most of them were drinking early because once the combination crossed the Kansas line the bar would have to close. He was glad Colorado had split off from Kansas just before the war. Save for electing idiots like Windy Howard Winger to public office, the voters of Colorado tended to show good sense.

As he bellied up to the bar and ordered a needled beer, a gent standing next to him, dressed more cow, said, "I can see by the way you telescope your hat that you're a Colorado rider, like me."

Longarm nodded but said, "I wasn't born in a bed of columbines, though. Came out here full-grown after the war."

His neighborly fellow traveler replied, "Do tell? I rid with the Colorado Militia under good old Colonel Chivington. You must have heard about us and the South Cheyenne, right?"

Longarm nodded and buried his face in beer suds lest his grimace of distaste show. The tracks ran not too far north of the one and only so-called battle Chivington's column had ever taken part in. Some of the Indian babies they'd butchered down along Sand Creek would have been almost old enough to vote by now, if Indians had the vote and got to grow up as often.

The erstwhile Indian fighter sounded a shade less friendly as he nudged Longarm and asked, "Which side did you say you rid for during the war, pilgrim?"

Longarm put his schooner firmly back on the mahogany, smiled pleasantly, but let his coattail clear the no-nonsense grips of his utilitarian .44-40 as he said flatly, "I never said. Are you writing a book or just naturally nosy?"

His tormentor glanced down at the serious hardware Longarm was wearing under his more sedate outer appearance, gulped, and must have decided not to torment him anymore. For he smiled sort of weakly, shrugged, and took himself and his own glass farther up the bar.

But Longarm had no sooner swallowed another mouthful when he heard the gent drinking on the other side of him chuckle and opine, "I never thought much of that glorious charge into that unarmed camp of tame

Cheyenne, either. My mother told me never to prod a stranger who looks as if he might be on the prod, either. But it does get tedious, just standing here with a lot of nothing much out yonder to stare at. Is it all right to jaw with you if I don't ask nosy questions?"

Longarm chuckled and replied, "You're on. What do you want to talk about and, before you start, what gave you the notion I'm on the prod?"

The other man, older, shorter, and less outdoors in appearance than either Longarm or the pest he'd just chased away, said, "Hey, look, if you ain't on the prod I ain't about to pry. I just thought, seeing we just left the Denver war zone, you could be as tense about things back yonder as the rest of us."

Longarm reached for two cheroots, handed one to the talkative townee, and said, truthfully enough, "I haven't been downtown for a spell. You say there's a war going on?"

His informative fellow smoker nodded as he struck a light for both of them, saying, "Yep. Started yesterday, behind the city hall. One of Senator Windy Winger's hired toughs locked horns with the one and original Longarm. You've heard of him, of course?"

Longarm didn't like to outright lie to innocents, so he just nodded and asked, "Who do they say won?"

A more rustic passenger who'd taken a space vacated by the first pest chimed in with, "Hell, Longarm, of course."

The more sedate gent on Longarm's other side said, "He surely did, and they do say the hired gun as started up with him was a pure professional."

The rustic snorted and said, "Ain't nobody shoots professional enough to mess with *Longarm*. They say that old boy once backed down John Wesley Hardin and Wild Bill Hickok at once. They was fixing to shoot it out one night over to Dodge, and since Longarm was the town law at the time, he just stepped between 'em and announced that the first one who drawed was dead. So they both lit out in opposite directions and everybody got back to drinking and screwing peaceable."

The one on the other side of the man they were talking about said, "I heard the same story, only it was Pat Garrett and Billy the Kid he stepped between whilst he was cleaning up New Mexico that time."

Longarm had to laugh. To cover it up he asked, "Do either of you gents know this thundering wonder?"

So, naturally, both of them nodded. The rustic said, "Sure. He's a big moose, even bigger than you, no offense, and he packs a big '45 on each hip."

"Colt Dragoons," the other gossip corrected, going on to say, with a little shudder, "They say he'd rather do an outlaw with that bowie knife he carries up one sleeve. Of course, Calhoun was coming at him with a sawed-off ten gauge the other morning, so Longarm had to just shoot him, a dozen times before he could hit the ground."

"Must have been noisy," said the only man there who knew what they were talking about.

"You can say that again," the townee said. "I heard it from my office on Colfax Avenue. Sounded like the Sand Creek Massacre all over again. They say right now Senator Winger is forted up in the Palace Hotel and sending all the way to Washington for more bodyguards. He must be scared as hell."

The rustic said, "Hell, yes, he'd be scared. Wouldn't you gents be scared if you'd crossed old Longarm and knowed he was stalking you with two guns and that big bowie? I heard that knife he loves to gut gents with was the one Jim Bowie in the flesh was carrying at the

Alamo that time. They say Longarm took it off a Mex officer he killed, bare-handed, later."

The other man said he'd heard that too. Longarm couldn't say anything without laughing like a jackass, so he just drank all his needled beer and ordered another.

But he didn't get it. For just then some fool pulled the brake cord and it was all Longarm could do to stay on his feet as the train wheels under him screamed to a shuddering stop. Most of the others in the club car, including the barkeep, wound up on the mighty wet floor. The pest he'd talked to earlier, wearing his hat crushed the same as Longarm's, was one of the few who'd managed to survive the sudden stop without landing on his ass. He moved over to the nearest window saying, "What the hell?" and slid the glass up to stick his head outside. Then a shot rang out, followed by a war whoop that would have done a dog soldier proud, and then the nosy cuss lay limp as a dish rag over the sill with his bottom half pissing its britches inside and the blood from his shattered skull running down the sun-baked, mustard-yellow siding outside.

Someone inside ye..ed, "Train robbery!" as Longarm drew his own gun and started stepping over lesser men, wondering what else might be new.

As he stepped out on the forward platform he had a glimpse of milling horseflesh, half hidden by churning dust, off to the left side of the tracks. He knew most of their riders, if they were really serious, would be up closer to the mail car, where the real money hung out. Few such gangs still went back to rob the passengers since the Pinkertons had taken to blending plainclothes gunslicks in among the sheep.

But whether he walked into less professional train robbers or not in the passenger coaches ahead, Longarm knew there were half a dozen infernal freight cars between him and the real action. He put his free hand to a steel ladder leading topside without thinking, then snatched it back as if the steel had been red-hot. For as soon as he *did* study on it, he saw how dumb it might look to run along the tops of the cars, skylighted both ways, to an undetermined number of obviously trigger-happy sons of bitches.

So he dropped into the narrow slot between the platform of the club car and the next. Then, gun in hand, he began a sort of three-legged crab walk forward, under the cars and of course between the steel rails and wheels, both offering him some cover in case he was spotted, with plenty of shade surrounded by plenty of afternoon glare, to make that less likely.

It took forever. The long crawl alone would have been a pain in the ass. But he had to slither more like a snake than a crab each time he came to a goddamned axle or brake tank, and it didn't help to consider if or when the fool train might start up again with him under it. But at last he was under the mail car and, sure enough, a heated discussion about opening the safe seemed still in progress. Directly under a wooden floor when a safe was about to be opened or blown, with blowing more probable, was not Longarm's notion of a safe place to be. So, while joining the party hardly seemed much safer, Longarm took a deep breath, rolled out just under the open doorway of the mail car, and began the festivities by blowing two nearby outlaws out of their saddles. He missed a third one riding off crouched low across the horn and bleating like a sheep. The mad flight of the fleeing train robber inspired others aboard the train to smash glass and throw some of their own lead at the others in view on the open prairie. So one went down, pony and all, and then the whole gang of, say, seven survivors was out of range, screaming defiance as they ran like rabbits.

Longarm had of course been too smart to expose himself to fire from the open doorway above him. He was flattened against one side of the car, covering the opening as best he could while he regarded the two blue-clad figures in the nearby shortgrass. Neither postal clerk seemed in need of medical attention. An undertaker could worry about them later. Longarm called out, "You, inside. I got you boxed and your pals ran off with your horseflesh. So let's proceed by tossing your hardware out to me."

A sad voice from inside called back, "We can't hardly do that, friend. I told the boys how dumb it could be to gun them old boys. But what's done is done, and they do say Colorado hangs a man for even stealing a horse."

"Look on the bright side," Longarm called back. "The gents you shot were federal employees and, by the way, I'm a U.S. deputy marshal. So we ain't talking about *Colorado* hanging anybody."

There was no answer. That was the trouble with letting owlhoots read. The one or more inside likely knew what a federal court dished out for murder-in-the-first or, hell, just robbing one of Uncle Sam's mail cars.

Longarm didn't think he'd better mention that. So he tried, "You say I'm not talking to the hand as pulled the trigger on these gents out here with me. Why don't you tell me all about it? Who shot these boys and how come?"

Another voice inside, making it at least two of them, sort of whimpered, "It was Red as gunned 'em when they wouldn't open the safe. That's him yonder, by that clump of soap weed. You must have been the one as shot him, mister."

27

Longarm nodded grimly, without glancing at the two he'd nailed getting out and up, as he called out, "It's good to hear I'm doing *something* right out here. Meanwhile, between us, we're sure messing up the timetable of the Kansas & Pacific. So how about it, boys? You know there's just no way in hell you're going to get away and, for all you know, some of the folk you're delaying in transit so cruel could wind up on your jury."

No answer. He heard the crunch of leather on railroad ballast and whirled, gun muzzle and all, to cover the already worried-looking brakeman edging his way, coal-oil lantern in hand. The damn fool signal light was as useless as the rest of him with the sun glaring down from a cloudless cobalt sky. When Longarm swung his gun the other way again, the brakeman gulped and said, "One of the engine crew got winged when they stopped us. He needs a doc. How long do you figure we'll be stuck here?"

It was a good question. Longarm murmured, "That's what they may be banking on. We could likely slide this door shut and leave 'em in there, armed and dangerous, until we passed some cover they fancied more than this wide-open stretch."

The brakeman said, "The old boy up in the engine cab is in a bad way, though."

Longarm nodded and said, "Give me your lantern." And, once he had it and could see it was really lit, he called out, "I just can't abide cruelty to animals. So I feel it's my duty to warn you animals in there how unpleasant the next few minutes figure to get if you don't start acting sensible. I got me about a quart of coal oil out here. I'm fixing to lob it in at you, which means you'll be coming out directly. I mean to kill anyone who comes out gun in hand. So make sure you toss your guns out first and—"

28

"Don't do it!" the whiny one screamed with what sounded like sincere horror.

His comrade yelled, "We got the safe all set to blow with plenty of nitro left over! You firebomb us we'll *all* wind up blowed to kingdom come, and *then* where will you be?"

Longarm growled, "You just said kingdom come, you asshole. I'm giving you one minute to come to your senses. Then we shall see what we shall see."

Then he turned to the brakeman and whispered, "Listen tight. First go back and uncouple the other cars from this one. Then run forward, on their blind side, and have the engine haul this one a good hundred yards before you uncouple it from the tender and put some distance between you, the engine, and it."

The brakeman started to ask a question. Longarm hissed, "Get moving, dammit! Didn't you just hear me give them no more than a minute?"

So the brakeman got moving and, although Longarm prided himself on being a man of his word, it was more like three full minutes before the car he was leaning against began to slowly move eastward. Longarm gripped a grab iron with his free fist and stood one booted foot on a truck rod, his gun back in its holster and the lantern swinging in his free hand as someone inside commented to someone just as mysterious, "Hey, we're moving!"

But that didn't work, either. A wiser voice yelled, "Don't go for it. There's no cover for miles and that lawman's doubtless still got us pinned down!"

By leaning out, Longarm could see they were now well clear of the main combination. He felt a jolt and now the car he was clinging to was slowing down again as the engine crew proceeded to put some distance between them the other way. So Longarm wound up, lobbed the lantern around the doorjamb into the darkness, and then, to make sure, slid the door shut and latched it from the outside before he was off and running across the dry grass in hopes of surviving the horrendous blast to come.

But it never happened. Longarm stopped on the rise he'd topped a good two hundred yards from the track to survey the whole scene in silent wonder. To his left the engine and tender had stopped about a quarter mile up the track. The longer and more-crowded cars of the combination reposed less restfully off to his right, with all the windows on his side open and everyone peering out and waving hats and such. In the lonely center of the scene the mail car just stood there, exhaling evil black smoke from every roof vent and up one crack of the door Longarm had locked the outlaws behind. Longarm lit a smoke of his own and waited. Then, as the smoke coming from the mail car began to thin, and damn fools from both the engine and other cars seemed to be moving in for a look-see, Longarm shrugged and mosied on back to see just what he had wrought.

As he got to a trio of men gathered around one of the two riders he'd downed, one looked up to say, "I don't know who you are, mister. But this poor dead son of a bitch is Lefty McNee, known to be a member of the Bacon gang!"

"Well, that sounds fair," Longarm said. "I'm a U.S. deputy marshal and they did seem to be robbing the U.S. Mails."

He moved on to the disputed mail car, mildly annoyed by the train of sudden admirers in his wake. He felt even worse when he heard someone murmur, "That's the famous Longarm. The government must have knowed the Bacons was out to stop this train today!"

30

Longarm slid the door open. Then he and everyone else had to step back, coughing some, as the thick black smoke inside rolled out at them. After a while, of course, it commenced to clear. So Longarm climbed in, gun in hand, to kick at the three bodies on the floor to see if anyone had any fight left in him.

There were no takers. As Longarm hunkered down to feel the throat of one, a Pinkerton agent he knew of old climbed in to join them. The Pink put his own gun away, saying, "Howdy, Longarm. I just heard you was aboard this combination. Up until then it was confusing hell out of me and my partner. Was all this smoke your notion?"

Longarm shot a reproachful glance at the burned-out albeit shattered lantern in a far corner as he replied, "It was. They told me a big fib. They told me a tale of safecracker's nitro and, as you can see, they were only bluffing."

The Pink chuckled fondly and said, "Hell, don't look so down-hearted about it, old son. I know you like noise. But think of the rolling stock you saved as you was, come to think of it, sort of smoking some Bacons."

There being at least a modest reward posted on each and every member of the Bacon gang, and whereas his Pinkerton pals felt sure one or the other of 'em must have hit that one rider Longarm hadn't, they agreed it was only fair that they take care of all the paperwork if he wanted to toss in the other bodies and the credit that went with shooting or smoking the same.

After that, things started going to hell in a hack.

The whole point of Longarm's mission to Stateline had been to hide his whereabouts a spell. So he was chagrined, to say the least, when they were met by a brass band and two carriage loads of scarlet women as their train pulled into the rinky-dink trail town later that afternoon. The infernal railroad had wired the news ahead of 'em down the track and, worse yet, got things all wrong, or, in other words, about the way they'd happened.

The spanking-new township of Stateline, as its name might indicate, had been organized a short spell back to take advantage of anything with money moving up or down the new Ogallala Cattle Trail, laid out along the string-straight border between Colorado and Kansas. The idea had been to avoid some of the noisy disputes along the older cattle trails occasioned by the conflicting claims and aims of moving cows and stationary bob wire. The hitherto imaginary line between the two states ran mostly across wide-open and mostly flat prairie. Washington had assumed nobody with a lick of common sense would file a homestead claim with, say, a hundred acres in Colorado and sixty in Kansas, for figuring state and federal taxes on such a spread would be a taxing chore indeed. But Washington had failed to consider how many ways there are to skin a cat, or the poor souls trying to make a living in the beef industry.

Stateline Township wasn't laid out exactly on the Ogallala Trail. Blocking free passage decreed by the government would have been dumb as well as illegal. Every ramshackle saloon and parlor house thrown up in recent months by money-hungry buzzards of all persuasions stood at least a few cow-widths back from the actual state line, making it, and the official Ogallala Trail, the main street of the town. So whether the town was in Colorado or Kansas depended on one's point of view. Since the state laws varied a mite on such matters as whoring, gambling, and even horse theft, the local notions of law and order were in a state of confusion the old gents who wrote the U.S. Constitution never could have foreseen, drunk or sober.

Like other such communities west of the Mississippi, Stateline had its own city ordinances, enforced by anyone tough or desperate enough to take the job. So while Longarm wasn't too surprised to learn upon his arrival that he didn't know the local town marshal after all, it didn't make him happy. Life was already complicated enough as it was.

He got away from the crowd around the railroad platform as fast as he could. There was another crowd in and about the nearby Western Union office. He didn't really need a haircut, and felt safer shaving himself than entrusting his throat to a razor in the hands of a total stranger, but next to a female sewing bee there was no better place in a small town than a barbershop to ask nosy questions. So he found a striped pole on the shady —or Kansas—side of the street, went inside, and when he saw there were three other gents ahead of him, sat down, picked up a tattered copy of the *Police Gazette*, and pretended he wasn't at all interested in all that ruckus down by the railroad tracks.

It worked. Two of the townees ahead of him were jawing about it to the barber, who, having missed the fun, kept asking questions as he went on smothering the customer in his chair with hot towels. The story sure had improved with the retelling. Longarm was reminded once more of the old saw about a jar of olives dropped at one end of town turning into a wagonload of watermelons by the time the tale was relayed to the other. But while the transformation of the Bad Bacons into the Reno Brothers and James–Younger gang, combined, was sort of amusing, it hardly cheered Longarm to hear the deal he'd worked out with his Pinkerton pals wasn't working. There'd just been too many others aboard that infernal train.

Somebody did say, mildly, that he'd heard the army of owlhoots had ridden into a trap set by the Pinks. But the loudest voice in the tiny shop insisted, "Bull squat. The deed was did, single-handed, by that famous federal manhunter, Longarm. He was laying for the rascals in the mail car, knowing they was fixing to rob it. They got his two sidekicks, but when they went to open the safe, old Longarm stepped out, both guns blazing, and wiped out the whole bunch."

The barber said mildly, "I heard one of 'em, at least, got away."

To which the man who knew it all replied, "He won't get far. Not with all them buffalo rounds old Longarm put in him."

The barber, who was old enough to remember, raised an eyebrow to ask, "Buffalo rounds, from this famous lawman's *six-guns?*"

The expert on such matters nodded sagely and confided, "Special ones, made to order for him by Colt of New Haven. They're on sort of beefed-up Dragoon frames, chambered .50 caliber, see?"

Another man whistled and said, "I'd surely like to see such light artillery. Handguns like that ought to kick like mules, or make that *elephants!*"

The know-it-all nodded and said, "Sure they do. That's how come he had to have 'em made special. It takes a giant of a man to fire a brace of .50s from the hips. But that's how come they calls him Long Arm, see? He's about seven feet tall or taller, with arms like apes have and hands as big as Virginia hams. I think he used to be a circus freak afore he took up the cause of justice."

A man closer to the real Longarm said, "You're

wrong. He was already a lawman when he shot it out with the owner of that Wild West show and circus up to the South Platte. He ain't all that unusual looking, just *big* as hell."

The barber asked if he'd ever seen the one and original Longarm and, while he had the facts of that one shoot-out about right, he had to spoil the real Longarm's opinion of him by going on with, "Seen him? Hell, I rid with him against the Shoshone, up to the South Pass a couple of summers back. We're good pals. He saved my hair a couple of times." Then, after a modest pause, he added, "I only got to save his life once. You're right about him being a dead shot with them .50 caliber six-guns. I seen him nail a Shoshone smack between the eyes at close to a quarter mile, both of 'em riding at full gallop."

The barber didn't argue. He asked, "Do you reckon he's here to pick up that one member of the Bacon gang they got locked up across the way?" And, to Longarm's annoyance, there was a hearty round of agreement. So he put his paper aside and stood up to softly say he'd come back when the barber wasn't so busy.

Nobody argued. He seldom struck strangers as a man to argue with when he was talking pure sense. But as he left, he heard one of them murmur, "Hey, you don't suppose . . . ?" to be answered by, "Hell, no, that old boy was big, but not half big enough, and he was only wearing one gun."

So, knowing it was only a question of time now, Longarm strode back to the Western Union office near the tracks. As he'd hoped, the train in all its gory glory had moved on and the crowd had about broken up. He went inside to find no others ahead of him. He tore a yellow telegram form from the pad on the counter and blocked out a terse message to his home office before he

told the sole clerk on duty, "This is a private but officious communication of the U.S. government. So I
don't want anyone blabbing about who sent it, hear?"

The clerk assured him all Western Union messages
were private, but when he scanned it he whistled and
said, "Wahoo! Wait 'til I tell my kids who I just sent a
wire to Denver for! But hold on. If you're him, I got a
message from Denver to *you*, Longarm."

He rummaged under the counter to produce Billy Vail's
wire and hand it over. Longarm took it with a sigh of
resignation. He'd been afraid the news had already spread
to Denver, cuss the hide of Samuel Finley Morse.

It had. Marshal Vail's telegram read:

NOW YOU DONE IT STOP MAKE PICKUP AND GET
BACK HERE YOU DELETED BY WESTERN UNION
SIGNED VAIL

Longarm shrugged and told the clerk to forget the
message he'd just been told to send. The clerk asked if
he had something else in mind. Longarm said, "Nope.
When the fat's in the fire there's no need to make it
sizzle harder." Then he shot a glance at the wall clock
overlooking the counter and decided, "I might be stuck
overnight if the big cheese at your town lockup has left
for the day. What's the story on hotels in this town? I
ain't been by for at least a month and they keep tearing
the place apart and putting it together again."

The clerk nodded and said, "That's for sure. Won't
be too many repairs called for until the next herd comes
through, though. In the meantime, if you're talking
about cold running water I'd try the Cheyenne Hotel. If
you're talking about hot running whores I reckon you'd
want the Prairie Dog Town. They're both just up the
way a piece."

Longarm said, "Cold running water sounds safer. How come they call the other the Prairie Dog— Oh, right, lots of holes. I'd best settle for the Cheyenne Hotel."

Chapter 3

Before he settled on anything for certain, Longarm had a good supper, consisting of steak smothered in hot chili beans, two slabs of apple pie, and three mugs of black coffee in the little eatery across from the town lockup. The little old lady who ran the place said she sure worried about serving such repasts to young men with big hats, but that she'd just given up on trying to serve salads and such to gents who insisted greens were what cows, not cowboys, ate. Longarm said he felt swell as he let her keep the change, helped himself to a toothpick, and headed across the wide dusty street cum cattle trail to pick up his prisoner.

That was when things started going wrong again. The deputy on duty was a young pimple-faced squirt old Henry, back in Denver, might have been able to fight to a draw, and, like that other officious twit, this one thought he was ten times smarter than any man or boy had the right or need to be. He didn't offer Longarm a seat. So Longarm hooked a rump over the corner of the deputy's desk as the little wiseass went through the motions of reading the onionskin his fellow wiseass in Denver had typed up. Then he sort of smirked up at Longarm and said, "This seems to be in order. But I fear you're just too late, sir."

"You don't have to sir me," Longarm said. "Just tell me how come I'm too late. Ain't the rascal still here?"

The town deputy waved a casual hand in the direction of the patent cells, which one could just make out through a doorway in the rear wall of the front and likely only office, saying, "Oh, we still got him. You just can't have him."

Longarm rose and stepped closer to the doorway, muttering to himself, "Oh, shit, here we go again," as he saw that while the cell facing the entrance was empty, there were three such send-away-for-and-put-together cages back there. The only one in use was occupied by a massive form, unconscious or asleep under a thin blanket aboard a bare spring bunk suspended from the boilerplate rear wall. There were no windows. The prisoner was dozing in an economy model, with all light and air provided by the cagelike, inward-facing end of the cubicle. The skinny young deputy joined Longarm in the doorway to say, "Don't wake it up. All it does when it's awake is beg for food and water or threaten me with a fate worse than death."

Longarm muttered, "Big Bob Bacon is big, all right. Get back to why I can't have him. Have you lost the damned old key?"

The youth led him back into the front office as he explained, "It's a matter of jurisdiction. Colorado wants him. Kansas says it has first dibs on him. I understand both are sending state troopers to pick him up, as of Monday morning. It ought to be sort of interesting when they show up for the same want, right?"

"Wrong," Longarm growled, "I got here first, and

I'm federal. So unlock that damn cage and I'll let you watch whilst I put the cuffs on him. My boss said to leg iron him but, hell, he don't look *that* big, and I don't have any leg irons to begin with."

But the young squirt shook his head and insisted, "I just work here, and I need the job. My orders are that nobody gets the big old bastard until our own J.P. decides the matter in our brand-new municipal court, come Monday morning at the earliest, so that everyone will have his say."

Longarm started to argue. Then he shrugged and said, "Well, I can see you ain't cut out to rope cows, and you ain't pretty enough to make it as a whore. So keep your damned job and where do I find your boss at this hour?"

The youth scowled and said, "He ain't in town. He rid off to his brother's spread to help 'em butcher some beef, and he said not to expect him this side of Monday."

Then he drew his single-action '74, sudden and showboat, to twirl it a couple of times by the trigger guard before he leveled the muzzle on Longarm's middle and asked, still scowling, "Do you still find me girlish?"

Longarm stared soberly down at the gun aimed his way to reply, not unkindly, *"Foolish* is the word you're groping for, little darling. Anyone can see you've been practicing in front of the mirror, but don't ever draw so dumb in the presence of anyone who might take you up on it."

The pimple-faced deputy looked as if he was about to kill somebody, bust out crying, or both, as he said, "Anyone can talk big, knowing I ain't allowed to go on and shoot him. But, fess up, ain't I got as fine a draw as need be, should dirty old men keep passing unseemly remarks about my figure?"

"Hell," Longarm said, "I just told you what a lousy shape you had, for a male or female. It ain't your fault they gave you a man's job before you finished growing up. It will be the fault of the asshole who gave you the job if you wind up dead before you wind up shaving regular. So put that fool thumb buster away and tell me where I can find the J.P. you mentioned."

The kid did no such thing. He said, "If you're so smart, why don't you scout up Judge Steiner your ownself?"

Longarm took a step toward the sass, growling, "Now you are starting to push your luck. I just asked you a question, polite, you little shit."

The object of his ire raised his '74 higher, gasping, "Don't you *mess* with me. I mean it."

So Longarm reached out to take the gun away from him. It was easy enough. He just clamped down on the cylinder from above and twisted, while the kid instinctively tried to cock the hammer to no avail. Once he had it away from the willful child, Longarm said, not unkindly, "It'd take a stronger man than you, or me, for that matter, to cock a single-action without turning the cylinder and, as you may have noticed, the cylinder won't turn while someone's gripping it and the frame at the same time. Do you want to tell me where your J.P. lives now, or do you want me to turn you over my knee and give you a good spanking?"

The youth gulped and said, "You won't find Judge Steiner to home at this hour. Try the Rainbow Saloon, first. If he ain't in there he'll be at the Prairie Dog Town. He's a sort of horny old cuss, as well as a widower."

Longarm thanked him for the information, handed

the old '74 back, and turned to leave. But he'd no sooner turned his back when the kid snapped, "Longarm!"

He turned to see that, sure enough, the fool kid was aiming that fool gun at him some more. Longarm sighed and said, "I sure hope you got that owlhoot's cell door locked. Otherwise he might come out here and challenge you to a game of marbles, for keeps."

The daring youth twirled his gun on its guard again to showboat it back in its holster, saying, "Good thing for you I was only funning. I've heard your rep. But rep or no rep, I'd have had you that time, had I pulled the trigger."

Longarm shook his head wearily and said, "Not exactly. You'd have been dead. For there are limits to even my patience, and you may have noticed I do wear a side arm of my own."

The boy grinned triumphantly and said, "Fess up, there's no way in hell even you could draw and fire in the time it takes a gun trained on you to fire."

Longarm started to tell him he'd thought to unload the kid's dangerous toy before handing it back to him. But the silly sass would only wind up loading the damned gun again, and anyone that stupid, wandering about with a loaded gun, made Longarm nervous.

The Rainbow Saloon wasn't hard to find. It was right across the street, and there was just enough daylight left to make out the streaks of orange, lavender, and spinach-green paint someone had defaced the otherwise tan falsefront with. A rinky-dink piano was in full cry inside. For a moment, as he entered, Longarm was inclined to fear, or hope, the notorious Red Robin was gracing the keyboard with her unskilled fingers and the piano stool with her skilled behind. But while it was a gal, and while her piano playing was just awful, it was someone else entire. He didn't attempt a look at her face as he mosied to the bar. Her rear view was inspiring enough. But while a romp with an old established pal was one thing, he knew he didn't have time for a start-from-scratch if Billy Vail had meant all those words Western Union had refused to dot and dash his way.

Since no herd was in town and it was that time of day most married gents were required to report in, the only other patrons seemed to be two cowhands and a gray old grump in a rusty black suit who looked more like Long-arm's picture of a justice of the peace. But, since he'd seen more damned taproom fights start with one gent asking another gent, direct, who the hell he thought he was, Longarm bellied up between the old man and the younger hands, told the barkeep he'd drink anything wet but liked a shot of Maryland rye and a schooner of beer best, and, when he got no argument about that, said, "I don't believe you was on duty the last time I rode through. My handle would be Custis Long. I ride for the Justice Department."

The barkeep finished filling his schooner, then handed it over without a fight and said it was all right if Longarm called him Kevin. Longarm downed the shot of what they expected him to pay for as real rye, discovered the beer, at least, was real, and was about to ask old Kevin if he knew Judge Steiner when the old cuss at his right snapped, "You can't have him."

That even surprised old Kevin. As they both turned to stare at the older man, he shook his head insistently and said, "I know why they sent you, Longarm. Kansas and Colorado are sending lawmen for him as well. I'll be switched with snakes if I can see who has the better claim on Big Bob Bacon. But maybe after I get a chance to read all your warrants Monday morning, we can work something out. It's a pure shame the stupid oaf wasn't born with three necks. But he wasn't. So I just don't see how two states and the federal government can all expect to hang him."

Longarm asked politely if he had the honor of addressing the one and only Judge Steiner and, while they both knew he could hardly be the tooth fairy, the younger lawman's respectful tone had a soothing effect on the cranky old cuss. He said, "The least I can offer is another drink, on me, once you swill the last of them suds. How come a man your size drinks beer to begin with? Don't it take you forever to get drunk that way?"

That was, in fact, the reason Longarm liked to sort of coast along on the rate his large frame could digest alcohol without it making him talk, or draw too fuzzy. But he knew better than to preach moderation to a gent with a drinker's nose. So he just said, "I'll be proud to have a drink on you if you'll allow me to buy the next round, your honor."

He wasn't ready to bring up the subject of disputed jurisdiction before they'd even swapped dirty jokes. But he did wonder, idly, what Billy Vail would say, later, if this other old fart ever said he couldn't recall signing any infernal release form whilst boozing with his old pal, Custis.

Behind them the piano player hit an off note that missed so wide it made Longarm wince. Judge Steiner muttered, "Oh, Lord, first my pecker and now my ears are going. I could have sworn that sweet child was playing 'The Gary Owen' 'til she wandered off into 'Army Blue.'"

Longarm chuckled and decided, "Sounds like she's trying to breed an Irish jig to something by old Stephen Foster. The final results ought to be interesting, if she ever gets it right."

Kevin the barkeep said, "Aw, give her a chance. She only just started here."

Longarm answered with a tolerant nod and Judge Steiner with, "Where was she working before that, the Prairie Dog Town?"

From the way the young gal's ears were blushing, Longarm suspected she could hear them, loud as she was pounding, cracks and all. So he tried to change the subject by saying, "This may not be any of my business, your honor, but I was over to the lockup just before I came here and, well, that one kid deputy they have on duty failed to strike me as the sort of guard I'd post on an owlhoot wanted by so many other courts."

Judge Steiner shrugged, belched, and said, "Young Jimmy does the best he can. He's the sole support of a widowed mother and we sent all the way to Pittsburgh for them patent cells. Big Bob is big, true enough, but not *that* big, and he's sort of stupid to boot. I don't see how he can hurt young Jimmy with them vanadium-steel bars between 'em. We paid extra for them bars. Ain't a hacksaw in the land as could cut through even one of them bars in less than forty-eight hours. It said so, right on the box they come in. Ain't no way in hell that big dumb Bob is going to get out of there before I figure out who in the hell has the best claim on him."

Longarm said, "I was thinking more along the lines of a jailbreak with outside help, your honor. I've reason to believe more than one of the Bacon gang is not only still at large but not all that far from here. They may or may not know Nasty Nate Bacon's baby brother is under the direct supervision of no more than one kid deputy. I suspect that if they did, Big Bob would no longer be with us. If I were you, I'd have at least three guards on duty over there with scatter guns, not one single-action '74 that kid doesn't know how to use."

46

The older man shrugged and said, "It's a good thing you're not me, then. The township can't afford that big a police force. It sure can get tedious trying to collect municipal real estate tax or even license fees in a town that can't make up its mind what state it's in!"

Longarm cocked an eyebrow and asked, "Don't you know which state government might have appointed you, your honor?"

His eyebrow really cocked when the old man answered simply, "I do. I was appointed certified notary public and justice of the peace by Perkins County, Nebraska, in the year of our Lord 1874."

Longarm had to have his second rye on that before he said, as gently as he knew how, "No offense, your honor, but wherever this township might be, it surely can't be Nebraska, and if you were appointed anywhere during the Grant administration—"

"Rally Round the Flag, Boys, and here's to U. S. Grant, the Savior of the Union!" the old man cut in. "Best damn general and best damn president *this* country will ever see!" Then Longarm caught him as he let go the bar and tried to sort of dive headfirst into a brass spitoon on the sawdust-covered floor.

As Longarm held him, Kevin vaulted the bar to grab the old drunk from the other side, saying, "He's all right. He does this every night, albeit usually a mite later."

Longarm asked where they were putting the limp deadweight, and Kevin indicated a corner table on the far side of the piano. So that's where they deposited him, as the piano kept on playing. The gal likely didn't notice, or care, how empty the place was behind her. As Longarm walked back to the bar with old Kevin, he decided it was just as well she practiced while not too many had to bear it.

Kevin rolled back to his side of the mahogany and asked if Longarm wanted another. Longarm shook his head and said, "Not hardly, thanks. I got to study on what that old gent was saying just before his lamp blew out. Is it your opinion the township of Stateline is governed by no more than a sort of ad hoc committee of expired J.P.'s, town lawmen who'd rather dress meat, way the hell out of town, kids not strong enough to support their mothers no other way, and so forth?"

Kevin shrugged and said, "Don't ask me. I ain't no lawyer. I've worked in wilder camps in my time. Such government as we may have seems to keep things running smooth enough, save when the herds come through. Then it's always every man for himself no matter how the city charter may read."

Longarm fished out a cheroot to light as he pondered the barkeep's analysis of the situation. Longarm was no lawyer, either. But it did seem only common sense that on a federal cattle trail, littered by a sort of squatter settlement run with no more proper paperwork than a hobo jungle run by tradition and common consent, the only lawman with serious authority was standing smack in his own boots!

He blew a thoughtful smoke ring before he looked for a roost to crow from, however. It was established common law that in the absence of a regularly constituted authority, the denizens of an unincorporated camp, or hell, a wagon train, had the right to govern themselves within reason. Just what that meant had led to more than one gun battle and many a necktie party. His orders were to bring Big Bob in alive, not get him or any federal deputy who might be in the way strung up by a mob. The mob was the basic political concept all other governments sprang from. Men and even a lot of women could act odd as hell when they felt a stranger was interfering with their homegrown notions of simple right and wrong and, dammit, the folks around here thought they *had* a proper town. So it could take as long to convince them of the error of their ways, without getting into a fight with 'em, as it might to just go along with the foolishness and work it out with those other real lawmen, once they showed up.

He left some change on the bar, said he might be back, and headed for the batwings, aiming to head back to the telegraph office. But just then the batwings parted to admit a weasel-faced gent in a tinhorn suit, clanging spurs, Spanish hat, and two Colt Lightnings, worn low in tie-down holsters, with the rig strapped on over the outside of his coat. Longarm felt sure he wouldn't want to wear his guns so serious on purely social occasions. But since it was none of his business, he made room for the odd-looking cuss to pass.

The stranger didn't. He stopped between Longarm and the door, looked Longarm up and down, as if he were checking a mental list, and said, half to himself, "Yep. You're him."

Then they both went for their guns. The stranger with the professional rig was good. Longarm had assumed he might be, when he made his own move a split second sooner. So while the would-be killer's guns both cleared leather before Longarm could fire, they only fired into the sawdust between them as Longarm shot him high, low, and sideways as he spun down on suddenly dead legs to wind up sort of pretzel twisted on the floor with his rump and pale face both facing the pressed-tin ceiling through the blue haze of gunsmoke.

The louder noise had at least stopped the piano and even woke up old Steiner. Kevin and the two cowhands had wisely hit the floor. Longarm told the chalk-faced girl standing bolt upright by the piano to do the same as, not waiting to see how well she took orders, he hit the batwings low and crabbed out of the light as he tore outside, gun trained on the world out there in general.

But all he saw to shoot at in the last rays of sunset was a spooked black pony, fighting its tether. One glance at the silver-mounted saddle and gussied-up Winchester stock told him all he needed to know, for now. He went back inside to call out, "War's over, ladies and gents. The law is already here, because I'm it. So the next question before the house is who was *he* and how come."

But naturally, in a trail town so casual about legal matters, a whole mess of nosy rascals had crowded in by the time Longarm had rolled the dead man into a more dignified position of repose and patted him down for I.D.

As Longarm rose back to his feet the young squirt from across the way tore in, waving that same old '74 about as he demanded explanations for the gunshots he'd just heard.

Longarm said, "I got things under control here, Jimmy. Meanwhile, who'd be guarding your prisoner?"

"He's locked up safe enough," the kid said. "I'm all the law there is when the boss is away, and I can't just sit there in the lockup doing nothing at a time like this, can I?"

"Sure you can," Longarm said. "Put that damn gun away, or at least get out of my sight with it. You're supposed to be holding a federal prisoner for the federal government, which is me, and this other dumb bastard here just found out how annoyed I can get at times. Do you really want me annoyed at you, Jimmy?"

Since Longarm had his own gun in hand at the moment, the kid just gulped and shook his head. So Longarm said, "Bueno. Get back over there and don't annoy me by letting my prisoner out before I'm ready for him, hear?"

The kid heard, and went. But from where he sat enthroned in his corner, Judge Steiner banged on the table with his fist and shouted, "Order in the court! I told you nobody could goddammit have that Bacon boy this side of Monday, and how come that other rascal's laying there covered with sawdust and blood, or is it blood and sawdust?"

Longarm said, "I just shot him, your honor. It was his choice, not mine. This wallet he was packing says he was a licensed private detective from Denver, name of Cyrus Dove."

He put the wallet in his own pocket, money and all, lest it confuse the assembly, and added, "With all due respect to the Colorado license bureau, that hardly seems fair. The name and surly disposition he just displayed goes with outstanding warrants issued by Fort Smith in behalf of the Indian Nation."

Old Steiner grumbled, "I don't care if he was an Indian. Did that give you any right to shoot him?"

"It sure did," Longarm said. "No matter what Colorado thought of him, he was wanted, federal, for murder and worse in the aforementioned Indian Nation. He wasn't an Indian, your honor. He just picked on Indians more than the law allows."

The barkeep, who'd seen it all, had no doubt seen enough of life to forget seeing anything. But the young gal who'd been at the piano with her back to the shootout felt obliged for some reason to announce to one and all, "It was a fair fight between an honest lawman and a wanted killer, for heaven's sake!"

Which encouraged one of the cowhands, who *had* seen the fight, to announce, "It's like Miss Etta says.

The one on the floor come in loaded for bear and spoiling for trouble!"

So his sidekick felt obliged to opine, "He found it, as anyone can plainly see. But yon lawman gave him an even break. The dead man said something too disgusting to repeat, even in front of a lady who must have heard it. Then it was *mano a mano* and, Lord, you never saw human hands move that sudden!"

The barkeep was finally shamed into saying, "The dead man went for his guns first. I can prove that, if I sweep some sawdust away. For he fired both his guns into my poor floor."

Judge Steiner decided, "That's a dumb place to aim guns. It's small wonder he wound up dead. But, all right, it is the opinion of this court that the poor dead bastard committed suicide by calling a man with Longarm's rep, and does anyone here want to argue about that?"

Longarm could have, since he was the only real law present. But he chose not to when everyone else agreed he'd performed a public service to the community and old Kevin said a round of drinks was on the house.

Longarm didn't join the stampede toward the bar. He was in enough trouble as it was. He slipped out into the gathering darkness to gather his thoughts. As he stood there, pondering his next move with considerable care, since all the moves he'd been making, so far, hardly jibed with Billy Vail's orders, a small shy voice asked, "What are you going to do now, Mr. Longarm?"

He turned to smile down at the little piano-playing gal. The soft light from inside made her even prettier and made her mouse-brown hair look more like chestnut. "I ain't sure," he said. "Everything I do seems to get me in more trouble. I was supposed to sort of vacation here incognito for a spell, only I keep getting more famous and easy to locate by the minute."

She asked, "Do you think someone sent that man inside after you, Mr. Longarm?"

"My name is Custis. I'm tired of talking about how I got my nickname. A lot of it has just been luck. But now Fort Smith is sure to say I tracked that rascal down whether he was after me or not."

The dead man's pony nickered. Longarm told it, "Don't worry. I was only cross with your fool rider, Blacky. We'll see about some water and such for you as soon as I figure out where *I* am."

The girl, Etta, asked, "Don't you have a place to hide out?"

He chuckled and told her, "It's not quite that desperate. If old Cyrus simply recognized me as a lawman who could have been after him, and then just acted natural, all I got to worry about is more unwanted notoriety."

She said, "He was dressed mighty fancy, and that bounty hunter's license reads more like a hired gun than a man on the run. He didn't recognize you and go for his guns, Custis. He sized you up, agreed with himself that you were the man he was looking for and—"

"You got mighty good ears," Longarm cut in, adding, "in addition to eyes in the back of your head, I mean."

She nodded and said, "A girl needs them, playing with her back to Lord knows who or what when a herd's in town. Pocket mirrors only cost a nickel and you'd be surprised what you can see in one if you prop it on the music rack next to your sheet music."

He chuckled and said, "All right. The thought had crossed my mind that old Cyrus had been sent after me. I suspect I know by who and, while I don't aim to fill your shell-like ears with dangerous knowledge, there's no saying who might think you know what if we go on conversing like this. So why don't you go back inside and see if the boys have any requests, Miss Etta?"

She asked what he was planning on doing. He shook his head wearily and said, "I ain't just keeping secrets from the children. I just got so many things I ought to be doing at once that I'm standing here like a fool instead of getting started. I reckon the first thing I ought to worry about is that poor pony. The late Cyrus Dove must have ridden him in from somewhere, and the next place in any direction is a good twenty miles or more."

As he stepped down into the dust to untether the dead man's mount she moved to the edge of the planks, asking him, "Will you be coming back here later?"

He replied wistfully, "That, too, as the only true law within as many miles as this poor brute carried such a morose individual, I got to tidy up, sooner or later. It just ain't true, no matter what Ned Buntline says in his nickel magazines, that some so-called code of the West allows you to shoot a man dead and then just ride off into the sunset, blowing down your gun barrel. I've never figured out that part about blowing down your gun barrel, have you?"

"I don't read those dreadful men's magazines," she said. "I'll be here when you get back. I may have some more sensible suggestions to offer about keeping you alive 'til Monday than blowing down a gun barrel."

Chapter 4

The colored night-hostler at the livery just down the way said it wasn't for him to say, but that the boss, come morning, would likely go along with Longarm's suggestion that they keep the apparently ownerless pony ninety days and then sell him for his keep if nobody turned up to claim him. As Longarm helped unsaddle the critter, the colored man asked what about the fancy gear that went with it. Longarm hauled the Winchester from its saddle boot, saying, "Waste not, want not. I never had time to pick up my own rifle, and a man never knows. The rest of this stuff is too fancy for my taste. But I'm sure some paid-off trail herder, heading back to Texas, ought to pay a fair price."

The colored man grinned and agreed anything they got for the silver-mounted saddle and matching bridle would be pure profit. Then, as he slipped the bridle to get some water and oats into the poor brute, he scowled, held the cruel Spanish bit up to the dim light and said, "I know it ain't wise to call a white man a cocksucker, but look what that cocksucker had in this poor pony's mouth!"

Longarm nodded at the spur rowel turning on the already cruel bit and said, "You're right. Lord knows what he meant to do to *my* cock if I hadn't shot him first. I'd get shed of that and sell the bridle with a stock bit. You got any?"

The hostler said, "Sure we do. We're cluttered up with spare horses and saddles. You're not the first gent who ever left a mount here and just left us to worry about watering and oating it indefinite. Riders get stove up, clapped up, or even shot up on the Ogallala Trail."

As the other man poured water for the black pony, who sure wanted it, from the way it commenced inhaling the same, Longarm mused half to himself, "Do tell? A man never knows when he might need a mount or more. What kind of money would we be talking if I needed a halfway decent pony and a scuffed up saddle in a hurry?"

"I'm not allowed to dicker," the colored man said. "I'd have to go with the bottom line my boss has set on some of the stock. I don't know what he wants for all the stock and gear on hand. But being as it's the slow season, I doubt he'd mind if I let anything go for prices I've heard quoted."

Longarm nodded and said, "Quote me down the middle of the road, then. I wouldn't want to waste your time, even if I had time of my own to waste. But what would you ask if I was to pop back in here sudden, asking you to saddle me a decent ride?"

The colored man shrugged and decided, "Two bits, saddle and all, my choice and cash on the barrel head?"

Longarm said, "Twenty five whole dollars would strike me as a mite steep if the results didn't carry me as far and fast as I might want to go. On the other hand, if you didn't try to screw me, I'd be too far off to argue about it when I got off. So hold the thought for now. Are you on duty all night or do I have to worry about starting from scratch if the notion occurs to me again in the wee small hours?"

The hostler said he didn't get off until well after cock's crow, his white boss being a late riser. So Longarm gave him a cheroot and headed next for the all-night Western Union.

It was still early night, of course, and so the same clerk was on duty. He said, "I have another message from Denver for you, Deputy Long."

Longarm said, "I know what it says and it can wait 'til I get one off to Fort Smith about their long-lost boy. I reckon I'd best discuss his bounty hunting license with Colorado, personal, when I have the time and a cooled-down temper."

He tore off a blank, and even as he wrote the message to Fort Smith in the legalese he'd learned from old Henry's rephrasing of his final reports, he muttered aloud, "You'd think even an infernal four-eyed paper pusher would think to ask a question or more before he issued a man from out of state a bounty hunting permit. Old Cyrus Dove didn't even fib about his name and the same name's posted on many a post office wall."

"He might have had political pull," the telegraph clerk said with a yawn.

Longarm said, "Bless your hide, that could be it. Nobody likes to argue when a lad shows up with a good report card from his teacher! I can't see many clerks at the license bureau wanting to cross a senator with a reputation for a bad temper. Even my boss is afraid to cross the mean bastard and I ain't sure *I'm* ready to, just yet."

He handed over the wire to Fort Smith and tore open Billy Vail's latest words of cheer. The wire read:

HOPE YOU AINT THERE WHEN THIS ARRIVES STOP IF YOU ARE HOW COME YOU DELETED BY WESTERN UNION SIGNED VAIL

The clerk said, "I have to read 'em when I take 'em down. So while it may be forward for me to say so, I'd at least answer this last one, if I were you."

Longarm said, "You ain't me, you lucky cuss. Nothing I could tell my boss right now would cheer him worth mention. So why waste a nickel a word on pissing him off?"

He glanced up at the wall clock. It was already going on nine-thirty. He muttered, "Shit, won't nobody be in any other offices I can think of, right now. Could you give me an educated guess as to whether a Kansas or Colorado coroner would be most interested in a cadaver spread out on the floor of the Rainbow, here in Stateline?"

The telegraph clerk shook his head and said, "It's a point to be pondered almost every time a herd comes through. Both the nearest county seats act as if they don't want to be bothered. There ain't a real county coroner within a day's ride either way, and the Baptists have donated a lot out behind their regular burial ground as a potter's field. I think the town clerk does write down the names before the carpenter and part-time undertaker plants 'em. Whether they get buried in a box or not depends on what they might have on 'em at the time of their passing."

Longarm reminded himself to put a few bucks he'd found in Dove's wallet toward at least a tarp as he mused aloud, "I thought Dodge was run sort of casual in its glory days, but this place has no more law than an infernal mining camp."

The man on the far side of the counter said, "Yep, Stateline is getting famous. Fast. Come sunup, that shoot-out you had in the Rainbow will appear in both the *Denver Post* and the *Kansas City Star.*"

Longarm nodded wearily and started to leave. Then he turned back with a thoughtful frown and said, "You know, try as I might, I can't recall discussing that matter with you up to now, and it only happened a few minutes ago. So how did you get so smart?"

The clerk looked smug and said, "News gets around, and most of it passes through my steady hand on the key. I've sent out six, no, seven versions of that fight so far tonight. You sure must be as good with your gun as I am with my telegraph key. For they say you put two dots and a dash in him before he could hit the floor."

"Who's they?" Longarm demanded. "And before you hand me that bullshit about confidentiality, I feel it's only fair to mention that I've had some lip on that before and that I always point out how much federal, repeat federal, open range your outfit has its wire strung across, with an interstate franchise that has to be renewed now and again."

The clerk grinned boyishly and said, "Hold your fire. I'm on your side. Learned my trade in the Army Signal Corps. The *Post* got the story from the blacksmith, who's a part-time writer and reports such local news to 'em."

"Who's the local stringer for the *Star*?" Longarm demanded.

The clerk thought and said, "That would have been old Jake, the barber. He says someday he means to write a novel about the way things really were on the old Ogallala Trail, once it gets a year or so old. They only print a tenth of the stuff he sends to Kansas City."

"I'm glad," Longarm said, "I noticed a lot of bullshit being slung about the barbershop this afternoon. That's two out of seven. Keep going as I cuss myself for wasting all that time over to the livery."

"Let's see," the clerk said, "young Jimmy, the deputy, wired a bleat for help to the nearest county sheriff, saying he was all alone while all hell was busting loose. They never answer. Then three cowhands in a row wired Fort Smith ahead of you to ask who got the bounty on Dove if *you* didn't claim it and, oh, yeah, there was a sissy-looking young gent I've never seen before who sent a simpler message to— Hold on, I got it here."

He picked up his own work sheets, leafed through them, and read off, "'Johnson, care of Western Union, Golden, Colorado. Dove dead. I told you so.' That's all he sent."

Longarm said, "I'd say it was enough. How long ago did you put that on the wire?"

The clerk glanced at the wall clock and replied, "Ten minutes ago. Maybe less. Is that important?"

Longarm sighed and said, "Not now, damn my consideration of dumb animals. What did this sneak I just missed look like?"

"I just told you," the clerk said. "He was a runty little gent, dressed sort of sissy for the Ogallala Trail, in a checkerboard suit and derby hat. It ain't bright enough in here to count every whisker on a man's face but, oh, yeah, he was wearing cowboy boots despite his townee outfit. I heard his high Texas heels clunking, coming and going."

Longarm half closed his eyes to draw a mental picture before he nodded and said, "Right. A short gent, dressed loud over riding boots. If he sticks around long, in a town this size, he ought to stick out. When's the next train through town?"

The clerk glanced at the wall clock again and said, "You can't catch the nine-fifteen no more. Next train won't come through before midnight, and it's an eastbound."

"Shit, was that last one westbound?"

"It was, and I follow your drift. If he sent that wire just before it came through, and he ain't still here in Stateline, how does Golden sound to you?"

"Awful," Longarm said. "I'd best see if he's still here."

The clerk nodded, but asked, "Wouldn't that mean he could be out to do the job Dove failed to do, Longarm?"

Longarm didn't answer. They both knew it was a dumb question.

Chapter 5

Even though he took his time and scouted cautiously, it took Longarm less than an hour to determine, in such a tiny town, that nobody but the telegraph clerk could recall having noticed such an outstanding shrimp and so, if he was still in Stateline, he was hiding like a cockroach in some crack. He wasn't registered in any of the few hotels or rooming houses in town. The gals at the Prairie Dog Town told Longarm they liked their men bigger and invited him to shuck his duds and stay awhile. Although he declined their kind offer, he felt it was safe to assume no derby was hung up in any of the cribs upstairs. He knew three of the whores from other trail towns and they were good old gals who'd cooperated with the law, within reason, in the past.

The mysterious gent in the checked suit wasn't locked up with Big Bob Bacon. Both the prisoner and his young guard were dozing when Longarm looked in on them, decided not to awaken either, and went across to the Rainbow Saloon.

Inside, he found the place deserted save Kevin the

barkeep and Miss Etta, who'd deserted her piano to jaw with Kevin at one end of the bar. As he joined them, Longarm noticed the center of the floor had been swamped and sprinkled with fresh sawdust. As he bellied up to the bar he said, "I could sure use plain draft. Nothing stronger. I'm already confused enough. I heard about your potter's field. But Fort Smith may want the mortal remains of old Cyrus, and it's a pain to dig 'em up again."

Kevin said, "Our part-time undertaker's ahead of you on that. He said he wasn't about to dig in summer-dried adobe afore he just had to. They got the cuss on ice and rock salt, pending further discussion with Fort Smith. Where you been all this time? You missed a hell of a lot of free drinks here, you know."

Longarm said he was glad to hear that and brought the two of them up to date on his more recent wanderings. Old Kevin just looked confused. The sort of mousy Miss Etta said, as if she had no doubt, "That innocent-looking one in the derby was their finger man. He must know you on sight. If he'd ridden in on a pony, like the other one, you'd have found it by now. So he came here from Golden by train and left the same way after he pointed you out to Dove and saw what a bad move that had been."

Kevin frowned and asked, "What's in Golden?"

Longarm said, "Good question. It's a sort of played-out mining camp at the base of Lookout Mountain, just a few miles outside Denver. They mostly brew beer there now. A spell back I helped clean out an outlaw gang that had been hiding out in them parts. The foothills of the Front Range are swiss-cheesed with handy hideouts. But I'm sure we got everyone connected with that earlier bunch of crooks."

"Hot damn," Kevin said, "they say the Bad Bacons

hide out mighty slick between robberies. Do you reckon the late Cyrus Dove could have been tied in with Nasty Nate Bacon?"

Longarm reached absently for a smoke as he thought about that, and then said, "If he was, a lot of yellow sheets sure need some rewriting. We had Dove down as an Arkansas boy who couldn't get along too well with Cherokee. It's true he wound up with a sort of casually investigated Colorado hunting license and the Bacons have been Colorado pests of late. But I don't know. Seems to me that if Nate Bacon had enough political pull to get official papers for his boys, he'd get one for himself and start robbing for high stakes, like any other crook with political pull. I fear I have reason to suspect old Dove was sent after me by somebody as mean but a lot more highly placed than Nasty Nate Bacon."

Etta said flatly, "Anyone who can hire one gun can as easily hire another, you know."

Longarm allowed he'd just said that as Kevin slid a schooner of beer his way. He inhaled some suds, put the schooner back down, and said, "Let's see, now. As I best recall the timetables of the Kansas & Pacific, I got until nine in the morning before the next train pulls in from the west. I might have even more time if the *next* one they send comes across the prairie the hard way, mounted."

"Why would anyone want to do a fool thing like that, Longarm?" Kevin asked. But it was Etta who answered. "For the very same reason that last one, Dove, did. It's one thing to just get off a train and gun a man. It's another thing entire to get out of town right after, when trains come through only now and again, see?"

Kevin brightened and said, "Oh, sure. Their sneaky lookout in the derby hat could afford to lay low and wait for the next train, like he done. But had Dove won, he'd have had to blue-streak out across the lone prairie in most any direction before the boys could make up their minds to do anything about it."

Longarm nodded. But the mousy little gal who seemed to know more about trail-town customs than piano playing said, "They know now, just as well as we do, that there's just no way a second killer can get here all the way from the Front Range by horse in hopes of finding you still here. If I was that mysterious mastermind in Golden, I'd send in, say, two or three, by rail. That scout in the derby would have told me the only law here right now, aside from the lawman I wanted killed, was a dumb kid with orders not to stray far from that lockup across the way."

Longarm nodded and said, "Right. Assuming they got me, and nobody can win 'em all, there's a whole livery overstuffed with horseflesh even closer than the railroad. Of course, once they helped themselves to mounts by broad daylight, getting away would be a mite more complicated—"

But she cut in with, "Pooh, who'd there be to stop them if *you* were down and that kid across the street was under his desk, bawling for help?"

Kevin said soberly, "She's right. You know how fond I am of you. But I, for one, would have a time convincing myself I ought to chase after anyone who'd just licked the one and original Longarm across open prairie with no cover to duck my poor head behind if they decided they just didn't *want* to be chased all that much!"

Etta said, "There's always that midnight train. It could have you back in Denver long before anyone could get here from there, come morning."

Longarm smiled thinly as he thought how interesting that could work out in the Denver Union Depot's waiting room. For the train she'd mentioned would put him there well before anyone could board the next east-bound, early in the morning. But he shook his head and said, "I can see the common sense in your grand notion, Miss Etta. But I ain't paid to show common sense. They expect me to show some grit when the occasion calls for it, and this occasion does. I don't know what anyone else that might be after me looks like. I don't see how I ever will, if I don't meet up with 'em *here*. So I ain't trying to be a hero when I say I'll have to pass on that midnight train. If they're after me here, they'll be after me no matter where I go. Waiting for 'em gives me an edge I might not have drinking after hours in the Denver Parthenon."

He drank another swallow in the Stateline Rainbow and went on to explain, "Even if it wasn't smart to wait 'em out here, I was sent here with more than that in mind. I can't go home without Big Bob, across the way. I can't have him, without a fight, this side of Monday. So, all things considered, I reckon I'd best hire a room for the night and sort of fort up until then."

Etta shook her head and said, "You'd best start closing up down here, Kevin. Custis, you'd best come with me."

He didn't know just how such a mousy-looking little gal might mean that. But since the hand she was leading him by was not his gun hand, he was willing enough to let her lead him through a bead curtain between her piano and the end of the bar. But as they moved up a dark and narrow stairwell he had to ask her, mildly, where in thunder they were headed.

She said, "You'll see." And, sure enough, when she opened a door at the head of the stairs and struck a light, he could see her private quarters, if they were hers, were laid out fancy as a New Orleans whorehouse, or maybe a brownstone on Sherman Avenue, since the vel-

vet hangings and gilt French furniture were sort of refined as well as expensive. She sat him down on a Louis
whatever love seat and sat herself down with him,
close, since that was the way such seats were made. She
said, "You really need a mother to look after you more
than that kid deputy across the way does. Nobody's
gunning for *him*, as far as I know. How long do you
think it would take those slickers to find out where
you'd checked in, if you were dumb enough to check
into any hotel or rooming house?"

He smiled uncertainly down at her. They were seated
close enough to feel each other's breaths, and he said,
"Not long. I was planning on getting up early to meet
that morning train. But I was still working on how I'd
know 'em, or spot an even slicker scout who might not
seem to be with 'em. Right now I'm even more confused about where we are and how come. Downstairs,
earlier, that barkeep told me you'd just come to work
here."

"I told him to say that," she said, "should anyone
ask. I *own* the place. I bought it a couple of days ago.
It's no secret to the town clerk, or even my close
friends. But do I have to tell you how much trouble it
can cause when cowhands passing through think a saloon is being run by a sissy girl?"

"Not hardly," he said. "Old Luke Short has told me
personal how much trouble he has running the Long
Branch in Dodge, baseball bat and all. But as the full
picture emerges from the mists, I'd like to know how
much this is likely to cost me. I'm only allowed a dollar
per diam, room and board, by my cruel-hearted boss."

She almost bit his nose off as she snapped, "Bite
your fool tongue!" and rose grandly to her feet. "This is
on the house," she said as she glided over to a sideboard
to build them both some drinks.

"Hold the thought. I've had enough to drink this evening, thanks. I may have had too much, as a matter of fact. For I can't see why you're being so good to me, Miss Etta."

She went on mixing her own gin and tonic water with her back to him as she asked softly, "Haven't any other ladies ever been good to you, Custis?"

"Some," he said. "But that was more like romance than a desire to get into a fight that wasn't their own. I suspect you know, since you've confessed to owning your own pocket mirror, that you ain't the sort of gal who has to risk her pretty hide to get your average man in a romantic mood, right?"

She replied, "Wrong," as she turned, glass in hand, to rejoin him on the love seat, adding, "I'd hardly call you an average man, Custis. But I didn't bring you up here to seduce you."

He muttered, "Oh, heck," and they both laughed. Then he took off his hat, took her in his arms, and asked just why she had.

"Down, boy," she protested. "We've got all night and, come to think of it, a whole weekend to think about that, if only we can keep you alive. I *want* to keep you alive, Custis. There was a time, and another man, when nothing I could do or say would help. He wore a badge too. I still miss him, terribly."

She raised her glass to her lips and drank from it, a lot, as he told her soberly, "There's been other times in my life, too. I reckon I've made a pretty lady cry now and again by passing up that tempting chance to settle down like a natural man. More than one has told me it hurts as much to have a lover ride out of their life, alive, as it might to bury him. But I don't know, I've been to too many lawmen's funerals to buy that. You ought to stay clear of lawmen, Miss Etta. None of us are worth a

69

woman's tears, and tears sort of come with the territory."

She said, "I know. Let's not talk about me. Let's talk about you, and how I might be able to protect you until the time comes for you to . . . ride on?"

He nodded and said, "We'd best discuss that, sort of man to man, or at least human to human, before that perfume you got on gets to me total. I can see you can see there's no future for the two of us past Monday morning, if I last that long. I'd be a liar if I said I wanted you to chuck me out like the brute I am. But I feel duty-bound to tell you that would be your best move. Nothing I could possibly do or say would be worth the risk you're taking in getting mixed up with me, you know."

"I know," she said. "Aren't you ever going to kiss me, dammit?"

He laughed, and did. Her drink spilled on both their laps as she clung to him like a limpet and tried to suck his tongue out by the roots. Their duds got even more disheveled by the time they were going all the way, or as much of the way as they could manage on the bitty love seat with so much infernal underwear in the way. As he climaxed in her that way, for the first delicious time, she moaned, "Oh, dear, you're getting ahead of me! Take me to bed so we can do this right, for God's sake!"

He did. He found it easy enough to pick her up and even walk with her with his pants around his ankles, but she had to point out the right gap in the drapes. On the far side he found a big four-poster. So he lowered her to the satin sheets and managed to finish undressing her without tearing anything, albeit she popped a button ripping his shirt off for him. Then they were down to just her black mesh stockings and frilly lace garters, and they agreed to let that wait until they'd done it right, old-fashioned and bare-assed across her mattress.

Later, as he lit a smoke with the pillows massed behind him to enjoy the sight of her sitting up naked, rolling her stockings down as she smiled sort of shyly at him, he couldn't help saying, "This is sure luxurious, in every way, honey. I know it's none of my business, but—"

"I've never been a whore," she cut in, adding, "I own a string of saloons up this cattle trail, now. I started with one my late husband bought in Texas with bounty money. We were planning on him retiring from the sheriff's department when he, well, went after one more wanted man."

"Hell," he said, "I never called you a whore, honey. Lots of gals screw fine, natural."

She laughed wildly and crawled back to climb on top of him, saying, "I could tell you were a man who'd know about such matters. Are you sure you don't find me a little, well, wild, once I get going?"

He assured her she made him feel sort of wild at times too. So she snatched the cheroot from his teeth, tossed it carelessly off into the gloom, and proceeded to get wild as hell, on top, as he protested, "Hey, for Pete's sake, let's not set the place on fire!"

But she said she didn't care if they burned to death, as long as they could die in orgasm. So he tried his best to pleasure her until he just had to roll her off, sobbing, and beat out the big burning hole in the rug with a pillow, tears running from his own smoke-filled eyes and unkind words streaming from his lips until at last he had the last sparks smothered, popped the window open, and said, "I'm sorry I called you a sex-starved firebug, honey. But, no offense, that was dumb as hell."

From where she reposed on the four-poster she

purred, "I've always enjoyed taking chances. Fess up, wasn't that sort of exciting, trying to come before the flames reached us?"

He climbed back in with her, muttering, "The damn smoke would have done us in first. You surely *are* a wild little gal, once you get started. I reckon you don't get started all that often, seeing there's only that one hole in the rug and no bullet holes in the wallpaper worth mention."

She snuggled closer to him and began to fondle his smoked sausage again as she purred, "I'm an atheist," as if that explained going loco en la cabeza in bed. When he said that was no excuse, she explained, "I'm sure we only get one short ride on the merry-go-round and so, while I have the chance, I want to try everything, see?"

He held her fondly, as any man would have, for there was nothing wrong with her petite naked body, but told her, "I can see you weren't waiting to take music lessons from the angels in no sweet by-and-by, but arson is only a thrill, if then, when you set fire to somebody *else*. I follow your drift about enjoying a short but active life, little darling. I read old Omar's Ruby Twaddle about having all your fun today because tomorrow might never come, and that's all it was, twaddle."

She began to stroke him harder as she could feel it rising to the occasion once again and murmured, "Pooh, I can tell a fun-loving man from a fuddy-duddy when I'm doing *this* to him. I'm surprised to hear you've read the *Rubaiyat of Omar Khayyam,* but if you have, I don't see how you can call it twaddle. *His* merry-go-round *did* run down, and all he has to show for it now is the fun he had while he still had the chance."

Longarm didn't really feel up to a philosophical argument, now that she had him almost up again, but he still said, "He was an infernal brag-ass, going on and on about raising hell with loaves of bread and jugs of wine like he was expecting to screw himself to death any minute. Only that wasn't the way he really acted. He lived to a ripe old age and held down a good steady job as the leader in Persian astronomy. For all his talk about tomorrow never coming, he knew the odds on it coming were a heap better than it not coming. He should have. He reformed the official calendar of the Persian Empire."

"He still died, in the end," she insisted.

He could only reply, "Well, sure he did. Nobody lives forever. But I've noticed folk tend to live a lot *longer* if they do consider tomorrow figures to come, a lot, until you run out of 'em."

She sighed and asked, "Have you forgotten who could be coming, tomorrow, on that early train?"

He said, "Not hardly. But whether I make it through tomorrow or not, dying of smoke inhalation tonight wouldn't have been any sensible way to kill the waiting time."

She didn't answer. She couldn't. Her mouth was full. So he let her get it up as far as it would go that way, and then they sure killed some time in a manner Omar Khayyam in full brag could have found no fault with. She even got up, later, to fetch a jug of wine, or a jar of gin, at least, for them to enjoy in bed together. He sipped his sparingly, not enjoying gin as much as most women to begin with, and wanting a clear head when that eastbound train rolled in. Old Omar had left out the hangovers one had to worry about when one guessed wrong about tomorrow and it caught up with you after all.

Etta was still following the old fake's advice, it seemed. She took four times as much into her much smaller body, saying it made her passionate until, after he'd passioned her some more around midnight, she just passed out cold while he was coming in her.

He rolled off, saying, "I've never been so insulted in my life," as he plumped up the pillow he'd slid from under her rump to lay her sleepy little head on. He liked his own pillow a mite less moist, bless her warm nature.

But try as he might, though his own pillow was dry and scented with lavender, he just couldn't get to sleep. Tired as he was, or knew he ought to be, he had more thoughts bouncing about in his skull than he knew what to do with. He knew it was a waste of time to go over the arguments he was slated to have with those other lawmen about jurisdiction. For he did that all the time on his way to the office back in Denver, and he'd long since learned that however he meant to explain getting late to work again, old Billy Vail always messed up his carefully planned conversation by saying something else entire.

The same thing went for who or what could be getting off that morning train. There was just no way to plan a fight when you didn't know who you might be fighting. His mind wandered back to the first real firefight he'd ever had, at a place called Shiloh. There'd been all them trees and stone walls no enemy had been hiding behind after all, and then, just as he'd started to figure it was just another dumb advance through empty woods, he'd found himself face-to-face with another young kid, looking just as surprised as he must have looked. He'd fired first, likely by sheer luck, and then it was load, advance, fire, load, advance, fire through a bewildering chaos of noise and gunsmoke until some damned somehow, the day was over, he was still alive, and tomorrow had come, just about as bad.

He sat up and rolled his bare feet to the charred rug.

She murmured, "Oh, yes, deeper," but she was only screwing in her sleepy head. She likely did that a lot, if the way she did it when she was awake meant anything.

He patted her bare hip and said, "I got to get it on down the road, honey," and, to his relief, she didn't answer. It usually worked out better that way.

Chapter 6

Owlhoot riders would have had to be called something else if they hadn't tended to sleep by day and ride by night a lot. So at one A.M., Big Bob Bacon was pacing his patent cell like a caged grizzly in stovepipe boots. Had he been wearing high heels the young deputy out front would have gotten no sleep at all. For in the interests of economy, the boilerplate cell had been bolted together on the original plank flooring of the frame building. The significance of this had been lost on the semiprofessional town law, and of course Big Bob was even dumber. So he was downright shocked and even a mite terrified when the flooring in front of him suddenly erupted in a fountain of splinters and flying planks. Big Bob fell back on his bunk to gasp, "Keerist!" as Longarm appeared from the waist up, with the rest of him standing in the crawl space under the not-too-solid edifice.

Longarm said, "Aw, I ain't *Him*. Let's go, Big Bob."

The gigantic moron was a slow thinker, as a rule. But he'd had lots of time and pacing to consider just how much he wanted out of the infernal old jail house. So he grinned like a shit-eating dog and leaped back up to drop into the hole in the floor with whomever this might be.

Then young Deputy Jim hove into view, looking taller from their vantage point, as he protested in a sleepy voice, "Hey, cut the stomping back there." Then he gasped, "Sweet Jesus!" and got his gun out, fast. "Now you just stop right there!"

Young Jimmy and his '74 looked like they meant it. So though his rescuer had already dropped down out of sight in the crawl space, Big Bob sighed, "Aw, shit," and raised his hands to just stay put until the kid unlocked the cell door to maybe help him back out. But then Longarm grabbed his ankles and proceeded to haul him down and out across the bare dirt as, on the far side of the locked bars, Deputy Jim kept cussing and clicking the hammer of his empty six-gun.

Once he'd hauled his prisoner out from under the rear wall of the lockup, Longarm reached for the handcuffs clipped to the back of his gun rig. But then he heard the front door slamming open on the far side of the building and so, seeing his prisoner was unarmed in any case, Longarm hauled him to his feet and snapped, "Let's go. I got two ponies tethered just down the alley."

As they ran for their getaway mounts and young Jimmy tried to wake the dead out front by bawling, "Jailbreak! Jailbreak!" the even dumber cuss beside him laughed and told Longarm, "I figured Nate would send someone afore them lawmen got here to carry me away."

Longarm replied, "So did I. Get on that bigger pony. I'll untether 'em both for us."

Big Bob did, Longarm did, and as doors and windows popped open all over town, they were riding out of it. Longarm led his want southwest at an easy mile-eating lope and yelled at him to cut it out every time he lashed his mount with the reins to go faster. He confused Big Bob even further by reining in on the second or third rise they topped to cock his head and listen. Then he said, "I reckon young Jimmy is having a time recruiting a posse to ride after the Bad Bacons in the dark."

Then he started to reach for the cuffs again. But his prisoner said, "That's for sure. But hadn't we best get streaking for the hideout?"

That was something to study on indeed. As best he could judge by moonlight, and allowing for having bought him the biggest horse the livery would sell on short notice, Longarm figured Big Bob had to be close to seven and change, and he was heavyset as well. On the other hand he was neither armed nor smart. So Longarm told him, "First things first, Big Bob. We want to put some distance between us and the sooner-or-later posse that ought to rise with the sun, at least. They'll be expecting us to beeline at a run. So let's just sort of mosey off at an unexpected angle and hope they don't have too many old Indian fighters to scout for sign across summer range."

As they walked their mounts down the far side of the rise, the big but sort of childish-talking owlhoot said, "I follows your drift. The dry grass is overgrazed all about, the dirt under it is hard as brick, and we just ain't *leaving* no sign. But you sure are a cool-headed cuss, considering how close we still have to be to that disgusting place you just busted me out of. How come you rid in solo and, by the by, who the hell *are* you? I'd likely recall such a distinguished-looking gent, had I ever met him in the past, and you know Nate never recruits nobody but blood kin to ride with him and us."

Longarm had known no such thing, of course. But he tried, "Some rules are made to be broken. You may have noticed I'm a specialist when it comes to patent cells. Of course, if you'd rather go back and wait for your *kin* to ride into a strange town whooping and shooting—"

"Let's just keep going this way," Big Bob cut in, as he studied some on the matter himself. Then he asked, suspiciously, "Where did you say you and my big brother, Nate, might have met up, ah . . . ?"

"Call me Moose," said Longarm, knowing he'd recalled the nickname a gal or more had bestowed on him for some fool reason. Then he said, "I don't know your brother and the boys personal. Like you figured, I was called in as a specialist."

"Oh, right," Big Bob said. Then he frowned and asked, "By who, if it wasn't by Nate in the flesh?"

Longarm shrugged and tried, "I'm good at forgetting names. Maybe that's why your kith and kin felt they could trust me. How do you feel about a short squirt who mixes derby hats with Texas boots?"

The big owlhoot pondered on that for a spell before he cheered up and said, "Oh, that sounds like old Stubby, a kissing cousin on Momma's side. You known him long?"

Longarm said, "I hardly know him at all," which was truthful enough when one studied on it. In case it might not be enough, he added, "Like I said, I'm a sort of specialist, not nobody's kissing cousin. I reckon your kin in the derby wanted you *out* more than he wanted you *kissed*. So he told me where they were holding you and sent me to fetch you. The rest you know."

They rode on a time in silence. Then Big Bob said, "It ain't that I ain't grateful. Two state troopers and a ferocious federal deputy called Longarm was fixing to fight over my poor doomed neck come Monday morning. But Nate's never broke the promise he made Momma on her deathbed, before."

Longarm replied, tersely, that he hadn't been there. So the overgrown kid, who had been, explained, "All the swell outlaws since Bobby Hood was betrayed, in the end. Momma said old Bobby Hood might be alive to this day if he hadn't trusted so many strangers. It's dangerous enough to take second cousins into your confidence when there's *money* posted on you. Even brothers has been known to back-stab one another, as it says in the Good Book about Candy and Apple. But you're just begging for a back-stab when you trust anyone you ain't even *related* to."

Longarm got out two smokes, lit them both himself, and reached one out to the bigger rider at his side while he observed, "I fear all them trusting gents you mention must have been before my time. I got your Candy and Apple figured out, but I can't say I ever heard tell of a Hood called Bobby."

"You're joshing," said Big Bob, adding smugly, "I'm named after him. Momma admired him as much as she admired Nate Turner, another tough old boy who got betrayed. Of course, that was before she found out he was a nigger. That's a good one on my brother, Nate. But don't never mention it to him. He gets nasty."

Longarm took a thoughtful drag on his cheroot before he asked dubiously, "Hold on, are you saying you could have been named after *Robin* Hood?"

Big Bob said, "Nope. Bobby Hood. He led the Greenwood gang over to Lincoln county somewhere back east in the olden days before the War Between the States. Him and Johnny Little, Freddy Tuck, and Red Wilson was at feud with the sheriff of Lincoln County, and had lots of fun making him look foolish as they robbed banks and stopped trains right under his nose. Momma said the Greenwood gang robbed trains even earlier than the Reno Brothers."

"I heard it was a spell back," Longarm said dryly.

Big Bob was wound up on the subject it seemed, as he went on to explain, "That old mean sheriff of Lincoln County never would have caught Bobby Hood, Momma said, if it hadn't been for a false-hearted woman he trusted."

"Maid Mary Ann?" Longarm suggested, with a thin smile.

His informant on down-home history soberly replied, "Not *her*, you idiot. They was married up and got along tolerable. The gal as done Bobby Hood dirty was a conjure woman, a Roman Catholic to boot, according to Momma. Them Roman Catholics have more healing spells than Gypsies or even Jews, you know. Anyway, Bobby Hood was feeling poorly one day, so he went to this old conjure woman for a healing. But did she heal him proper? She did not. She slashed his wrist and bled him to death for the reward on his poor head. Ain't that a bitch?"

Longarm managed not to laugh, which wasn't easy, as he said, "I had a false-hearted woman try to poison me a spell back. I think she was a Methodist, though."

Big Bob nodded and said, "I'll bet she was no kin of yours, right?"

Longarm said, "By gum, now that I study on it, she sure wasn't. I wish I'd had a momma smart as your own, Big Bob."

That got his prisoner, who still didn't know he was a prisoner, to talking down-home indeed, and as they rode ever onward in the moonlight, he learned a lot more about the Bacon gang than anyone had ever managed to tell him before.

It was small wonder so little was actually known about the inbred if not incestuous outlaw clan. Like the Renos and James-Younger gang, the Bacons and a few in-laws they'd been forced to breed with, when there just weren't enough kid sisters to go around, had apparently been raised as secretive criminals, suspicious of even their neighbors, since Great Grandfather Bacon had gone over the hill from the British Army during or shortly after the Battle of Saratoga. After a generation or so spent as the original cowboys, as cow thieves were once called in the tangle woods of York State and Vermont, the inbred clan had followed the wagon trains west, not to look for gold but to steal it. Without pressing the matter, but encouraging Big Bob to ramble on, Longarm was able to learn the current generation of the outlaw trash had been raised, if that was the proper term, by a momma and more than one kissing cousin in what had to be a secluded valley in the Front Range, just west of Denver. On her deathbed, after introducing Nasty Nate to sex as well, Longarm suspected, the vicious illiterate matron of the tribe had named Nate leader and filled his young head with a bitter hatred as well as suspicion toward just about anyone she'd never screwed, personal. Longarm had to admit that might be a good way to raise a gang of mad-dog outlaws if you didn't want to make it easy for the law to infiltrate them. According to Momma, a man was a fool to trust the mother of his children if he didn't know how much bounty money there might be on *her* folk. From a few other casual references to the hideout the law had scouted high and low for to no avail, some more socially acceptable but nontheless crooked kin were fronting for the wolf pack as official owners of the property, posted against trespassers. It sounded simple. But it made sense. Few casual hunters or stock grazers would be apt to defy the owners of posted property in the Front Range foothills with so much unposted range free for the wandering. Naturally, few posses would be stopped by a No Trespassing sign on a mere bob wire fence. But just as naturally they'd hesitate to cut the wire if they knew, or thought they knew, the honest owners well enough to take their word there was nothing worth searching for on the spread. Even Big Bob would know better than to leave a clear trail through a fence. When Longarm risked allowing as much, Big Bob grinned know-it-all and said, "Sure, you just have to follow the regular wagon trace as passes the front gate and just open it. Once it's locked behind you, nobody ever follows without asking our more stuck-up cousins permit. It says right in the county clerk's book that it's a mineral claim, and everybody knows how testy some folk deal with suspicioned claim jumpers. Hell, Nate shot one old nosy gent *lawfully* just about a year ago for just reining in to read the sign out front. Of course, our kin raised pure ned about that. Had to haul him inside the fence before they notioned the sheriff about it."

Longarm asked, "Didn't the county want to sort of look around inside, once they came to gaze on the grim results?"

"Sure," Big Bob said. "That's why Nate got fussed at. We all had to ride way up the valley and lay low a spell. It was raining and we all got ticks, hunkered in the aspen all the durned day. But the law was content to poke about the claim a few minutes and have some coffee and cake with our cousin and her man, a cousin she's got wrapped around her finger." Then he suddenly stopped, turned in his saddle to stare soberly at Longarm, and asked, "Hey, are you trying to pump names and addresses outta me, Moose?"

Longarm said, "Not hardly. I never even asked about

Candy and Apple. If you're worried about me being a Pinkerton man, what say we just split up, right here? I done what I was sent to do. It's no concern of mine where you might or might not want to go from *here*." He waved his free hand at the starry horizon to the southwest and added, "I'm headed for a hideout of my own, not near as far. It's got cover and running water and, the last time I looked, nobody else was using it. I'll just hole up there during the coming daylight hours. You go on home to your mysterious home spread if you want. Like I said, I'm good at forgetting names and places. So it's been nice talking to you."

As they rode on, Longarm noticed Big Bob still seemed to be with him. The big dumb owlhoot protested, "Hold on, now, dammit. We're a good four nights' ride from the Front Range and I am pure destitute of arms or even eating money!"

Longarm said, "More like five or six nights on the trail, my smarter way. I only got one side arm and I may need this Winchester if half the things they say about the tracking skills of that ferocious Longarm is true. But I can spare you a few bucks if that'll carry you home. I got paid in advance for this night's work and, like you said, maybe it's best we forget we ever met up. I don't think even that young deputy back there got a good look at *my* face, so—"

"Now just you cut that out!" the confused giant cut in, adding, "I never said you was no Pinkerton man, dammit. Why in thunder would Cousin Stubby hire a Pinkerton man to spring me outta that there jail back there?"

Longarm shrugged and said, "You got to watch out for those sneaks. Like you said, we ain't kin. For all I know, *you* could be a lawman working undercover, right?"

Big Bob gasped, "Now you're really talking crazy! Everybody knows who *I* am, damn your eyes!"

Longarm shook his head and said, "I never laid my damned eyes on you 'til tonight. It's true the Bacon gang just stopped a train not too far from here, dumb. It's true the law was said to be holding Big Bob Bacon in Stateline, and I can't see our mutual pal, Stubby, hiring me to rescue a lawman instead. But suppose someone like that sneaky Longarm found out about our plans and . . . you know, come to study on it, they do say the one and original Longarm is a big stupid-looking rascal."

Big Bob said, "Oh, for God's sake, you can't be dumb enough to think I could be Longarm, out to trick you!"

The real Longarm said, "I'll allow I could be stretching the possible suspicions a mite. But what the hey, let's say I just give you a ten-dollar gold piece to keep and cherish. Then we'll just part friendly and say no more about it."

Big Bob wailed, "You can't desert me on the lone prairie like this! It's inhuman! You was paid to get me home safe, not hung like a dog by them trail herders hot on our trail by now!"

Longarm made a great show of reaching in his change pocket as he said, "They ain't after *me*. They're after *you*. But I'd have a time explaining that if they caught up with me in your company. It ain't that I don't like you, you suspicious cuss. But I'll be damned if I'll take any more chances for anyone I ain't related to, neither."

Big Bob said stubbornly, "Like it says in the Good Book, wherever thou art headed, I'm riding with you. So where are we headed, Cousin Moose?"

• • •

They couldn't make it in one night, given such a late start. But as the rising sun caught them out on the open sea of grass, able to see for miles, with nothing that looked at all like a posse, or even its dust, Longarm pressed on with his prisoner riding at his side, still blissfully unaware he was a prisoner.

Daylight did nothing to improve the appearance of either of them. Longarm was dusty and in need of a shave. Neither hours in a barbershop nor a thirty-dollar suit would have disguised the fact that Big Bob was ugly as sin. Despite his status in the Bacon clan as the baby brother, he looked a lot older and meaner than the twenty-two years his yellow sheets gave him. His close-cropped head and unshaven face rose from his greasy gray work-shirt collar on a neck bigger around than the waistline of Miss Etta back in Stateline. Longarm wondered wistfully if she was starting to miss him as much as he missed her right now. Turning his thoughts back to Big Bob, he considered how little the giant was wearing, because they'd taken away his hat, guns, belt, and would have taken away his shoelaces if they hadn't arrested him in those low-heeled boots. Longarm wore old army boots with low heels because he spent more time on his feet than your average cowhand, and knew better than to shove a whole foot through a stirrup, falling off, in any case. When he commented on his fellow traveler's low heels, Big Bob said that was Nasty Nate's notion. He'd said his baby brother stood out enough in crowds as it was. Longarm noticed he rode well enough for such a big, clumsy-looking cuss, but they still had to stop and rest their mounts more often. The gray Longarm had bought off the night man at the livery was almost two hands higher than the roan mare he'd chosen for himself, but it still had a chore taking Big Bob up a rise at even a trot.

By now they'd become so friendly that Longarm was tempted to press his prisoner for more details. But an even sneakier plan was forming in Longarm's mind, and it might not work if the moron knew right off that his rescuer didn't have the notorious gang's mysterious hideout pinpointed on any map.

When at last they spotted cottonwood tops ahead, Longarm reined them to a casual walk and said, "Them trees are growing along Sand Creek. The Indian agents ain't made up their minds about Sand Creek. They got it set aside for South Cheyenne, if they could get any South Cheyenne to come back. Meanwhile, this stretch ain't open to homesteading. There could be someone grazing stock in such surroundings, though. So let's just ease in polite and see what's what."

The ponies caught the scent of greenery and water ahead, and wanted to get there quicker. Longarm yanked back on his reins and insisted, "I said *ease* in, ma'am!" He saw his prisoner had his own mount under control as well, thirsty as it had to be by now.

They topped the last rise to gaze down into the wide, sandy draw where once Indian children had played, and died, in the sunset of an era the Indians called the Shining Times. The shallow creek still ran cool and clear. Tall cottonwoods and shorter crack willow and wild cherry still grew there, maybe thicker now than when old Black Kettle's band had been camped there at peace, with the Red, White, and Blue fluttering above the chief's lodge.

Half to himself, but aloud, Longarm said, "The riders under that butchering Colonel Chivington must have formed about here for their charge. They say some of the kids were waving to 'em as they came down off this rise. They didn't open fire 'til they were almost smack on top of the unsuspecting Indians."

Big Bob said, "I heard about the Battle of Sand Creek when I was little. I fail to see why you seem to side with the infernal redskins, Moose. Ain't it a plain fact that later, on the Washita, Custer rescued white gals being held by the very same band of South Cheyenne?"

Longarm nodded and said, "He did, and they say one of the white captives is still locked up in an insane asylum back east. There's no argument about how mean and ugly Black Kettle and the other survivors of this earlier fight got, once it was over. Let that be a lesson to you, Big Bob. Never leave a man alive after he's seen you rape his woman and cut up his kids with a saber. The brave Colonel Chivington had himself a tobacco pouch made from the tanned scrotum of a Cheyenne they castrated still half-alive, and all his men took hair, speaking of how mean men can get." Then he pointed up the draw a ways to add, "Would you say that was wood smoke yonder, past that lightning-struck cotton-wood?"

His prisoner stared thoughtfully at the barely visible haze of wood smoke to opine, "I would. Small fire, like a cow thief running brands might make. You'd best hand over that Winchester now, Cousin Moose."

Longarm had been worried about something like that coming up sooner or later. But he had to agree nobody with a lick of sense would just ride in like a big-ass bird. So he grudgingly hauled the Winchester he'd taken off one killer, handed it to the other killer, and said, "Stay here to cover me. By now they've seen us, unless they're blind as bats. I'll ride in more politely armed. If they're dumb enough to pepper a rider covered by a rifle, you'd best head somewhere else, hear?"

Big Bob started to lever a round into the chamber,

but Longarm warned, "Don't. I'll tell you when I want brass wasted in the grass, old son."

So Big Bob just cocked the rifle with a grim nod, and Longarm rode down the slope at an angle, listening for unfriendly sounds behind as well as in front of him. But Big Bob didn't try to shoot him in the back with the recently unloaded Winchester Longarm had just entrusted him with, and as he neared the green tangle the smoke was rising from, a female voice called out, "Don't shoot! We mean no harm to you or your people!"

Longarm reined in to call back, "Come on out, then," and two women stepped shyly into view, holding their skirts up to let him see they were both really women. He saw, in addition to their pubic hair, that he'd been right about that mission-school accent. He told the Cheyenne-beaded girls he was satisfied of their innocent intent. So they dropped their deerskin skirts to a more modest position, sort of blushing, thanks to some of the talk they'd heard from the same white teachers they'd learned English off of.

Longarm didn't wave Big Bob in until he'd ridden between the two obviously unarmed Indian gals to scout their camp better. He saw two ponies and only two ponies browsing cherry twigs on the far side of the tiny cooking fire. A black pot was simmering on the coals. There were two and only two bedrolls in sight. He moved back to where the other white man on the rise could see him better, then waved him on in.

As Big Bob rode down the slope toward them at a thoughtful walk, Longarm turned in his saddle to ask the nearest Cheyenne maiden where the rest of her band might be. She looked down at the sand between them and murmured, "Back at the reserve, many miles from here, we hope. I am Corn Burner. This is my sister, Bad Baskets. We don't want to marry a fat old man our people say we should. So we came here, to this bad place, to hide. Last night we were too frightened to sleep without a fire. There are many spirits here. Have you eaten?"

Before Longarm could answer, Big Bob joined them, holding out the Winchester with a puzzled expression as he said, "You know what you just done, Cousin Moose? You left me to cover you with no rounds in this fool magazine, that's what you just done!"

Longarm took it from him, muttering, "Do tell? I was sure I'd reloaded last time I cleaned her." Then he pretended to be chagrined as he worked the lever a couple of times, swore softly, and said, "Well, I never. That's one on me all right, and it's sure lucky for me these gals are friendlies." He put the Winchester back in its boot, pointing to the gals on the ground as he said, "Big Bob, meet Corn Burner and Bad Baskets." He was too polite to say Corn Burner was the pretty one with trim ankles or that Bad Baskets was the fatter and uglier one. It would have been just as impolite to explain how Indians tended to name their kids with simple justice, rather than after someone already established as to character. The names of the runaway gals, along with why they might not have gotten on so well at home, were self-evident. He did say, "They want to know if we've eaten. That's an invite to dismount and stay a spell. But mind your manners and don't eat too much."

As the two white men dismounted, Big Bob sort of growled, "I could eat a horse right now. But after all that time locked up with just my fist for company, the big one's *mine*."

Longarm didn't answer. He could see they were already making the two young gals sort of anxious. He'd have been satisfied to give Big Bob old Bad Baskets and keep pretty little Corn Burner, if that was all there was

91

to it. But as a federal officer he felt obliged to remember Indians were wards of the federal government, and that raping one called for twenty-at-hard, minimum.

Whether they felt like getting raped or not, the two young wayward gals rustled up some tin plates and ladled out some of their fine gray mush for their honored guests.

As all four sat around the fire, Big Bob picked dubiously at his portion and growled, "What is this shit? It looks like parched corn with cherries and grass in it!"

Longarm said, "You got good eyes. That's about what it is. But don't be so suspicious, it ain't bad."

He was being polite, of course. A lot of Plains Indians were of the opinion Caucasian cooking was just awful. Captured hostiles were forever starving their fool selves to death under the mistaken impression their white captors were trying to poison them with army rations. It was all in the way one had been weaned off Momma's breast, Longarm figured. Both sides felt sure food ought to taste and smell the way Momma had always served it. He no longer minded sweet-grass seasoning, and neither stewed wild fruit nor boiled corn tasted all that bad if you sort of pushed 'em apart with your spoon to try one or the other. As he saw Big Bob still hesitating, he murmured, "Don't be impolite. It won't hurt you as much as it might hurt them if you turn up your nose at food offered friendly. If you think *this* tastes odd, wait 'til you try broiled buffalo tongue with maple sugar over it."

Big Bob grimaced and dug in since he really was hungry. So the two young gals exchanged relieved glances. Corn Burner said, "I wish we *did* have some maple sugar to put in with the sweet grass. I've only tasted it once. The old ones say that in the Grandfather Times we used to get lots of maple sugar from the woods we lived in before you people pushed us out on the plains. In the Shining Times we still got some from the Chippewa or Cree, far to the north. We got along better with them than our Lakota friends. We spoke almost the same tongue."

Bad Baskets rubbed her fat tummy as she added, "Wild rice, too. I've *had* wild rice. Yum yum yum."

Big Bob grinned at her but muttered to Longarm, "I got something yummy for her, balls and all. We've et enough of this shit to be polite. When do we get down to some *fun?*"

Longarm growled, "Dammit, Bacon, they both speak English. Let me do the talking, you uncouth rascal."

He turned to Corn Burner and said, "Hear me. My friend and I have run away from our band too. We mean to camp here, in this spirit place, until the owl hoots some more. My friend thinks your sister is very pretty. He would like to play his nose flute outside your father's lodge. But he hasn't got one, and I doubt your father would go for it, in any case. He's not trying to scare the rest of us with his rough manners. He's just not used to courting anyone more refined than a grizzly sow in heat."

The one he was talking to said something to her sister in their own mixture of growls and chirps. Bad Baskets said something that sounded even dirtier and they both giggled. Then Corn Burner asked Longarm if he thought *she* were pretty. So, since that twenty years at hard only applied when a ward of the government seemed unwilling, he said he surely did. But when she suggested they go for a stroll to carry on the conversation more privately, he gulped and said, "Hold on, honey. I like to stroll as much as most men. But does your sister understand my friend may not be noted for his manners?"

She giggled again and talked Cheyenne at Bad Baskets some more. It was a tricky lingo. Even other nations who spoke Algonquin said Cheyenne talked sort of funny. That was what Cheyenne meant. But he hardly needed a translator when he picked up a couple of mighty shocking words he knew for sure. Bad Baskets laughed and burbled back just as sassy. So Longarm didn't argue when the one with him said, "She says she wants a good fuck too."

He just rose with her, both ways, and let her lead him by the hand until they were out of sight of the others and standing in sweet grass, shaded from the late morning sun and even nosy eagle birds by fluttering green leaves. She said, "I am glad you think I am pretty. I think you are pretty too." Then she slipped her simple deerskin garment up over her braided black hair and fell to the sweet grass wearing nothing but her braids, mocassins, and mighty friendly smile.

Longarm took longer to get undressed, having more on to begin with, but once he was as bare as her, he made up for it by dropping into her welcoming arms and lusty love saddle. He was pleasantly surprised by how sweet and tight she felt, when one considered how hard she made a man fight to get in her. He wondered if the time would ever come when white gals learned to keep such things so simple. He didn't make the mistake of despising the pretty little thing for being so easygoing. He knew her kind could fight like wolverines if they didn't really like a gent. She and her sister had gone to a heap of trouble to avoid the advances of a man neither fancied. So he took her willingness as a compliment and, from the way she responded to his carefree lust, he assumed she felt complimented too.

He didn't kiss her and he didn't ask what she thought she was doing when she began to pant in his face like an out-of-wind puppy. He knew her kind considered that romantic, like blowing a turkey-bone flute with one nostril. He got her legs as high and as far apart as they'd go, but didn't suggest any odder positions once they'd climaxed together the first time. For while white gals enjoyed contortions, once they got around to it at last, her kind liked to keep their screwing simple and direct, if the one on top was up to it. She gasped, "Oh, you do it so good and so fast. Do you have many wives at home?"

He didn't answer. He just panted back at her as he kept on pounding her brown rump into the sweet grass. If her band was still polygamous he saw no need to confuse her pretty little head about stuffy Christian notions. Even white gals found his own views on marriage, multiple or otherwise, a mite confusing. She decided, "Yes, you must have many women, many, and I am so happy I met you when you were pining for them all. I have not done this either for many nights, many. Do it faster, harder, make me feel like many women doing it with you at the same time!"

He would have. But then they heard an anguished scream and Corn Burner stiffened under him, gasping, "That is my sister! What is your friend *doing* to her?"

Longarm rolled off her and sprang to his feet, stark naked, to find out. As he tore back to the fire through the whipping brush, he took in the situation at a glance and called out, "Cut that out, you damn fool!"

But Big Bob was in no mood to listen as he sprawled atop the fat gal he'd pinned facedown in the dust. They were both naked, too. So there was no mistaking where the giant had his big old tool as Bad Baskets hammered the sand with her clenched fists, tears streaming down her broad brown cheeks as the huge white man kept sodomizing her, unaware or uncaring as blood and worse kept squirting out between them with each savage thrust.

Longarm grabbed the moron's bullet head in both hands and twisted his thick neck, shouting, "Stop it! Can't you see you're hurting her!"

But Big Bob was maddened by lust and kept right on abusing her, growling like an animal until, suddenly, Longarm felt a sharp snap and Big Bob went limp enough for him to haul the big bare carcass off the Indian gal, easy.

As Bad Baskets rolled way, one hand to her torn-up behind, crying fit to bust, Corn Burner caught up with Longarm, who now stood staring morosely down at what was left of Big Bob. As Bad Baskets wailed at them both in Cheyenne, Corn Burner gasped and said, "Oh, she says he forced it up her, and just *look* at how big that thing is, even soft! Hit him again! He was very wicked!"

Longarm sighed and said, "Lord knows he has another lick coming. But he wouldn't feel it. I fear I just broke his fool neck."

The naked girl dropped to her knees to peer deeper into Big Bob's half-open eyes. Then she said, "You are right. He is dead. Now what are we to do?"

Longarm said, "You gals don't have to do nothing. I got to bury him. I sure wanted to talk to him some more. But, what the hell, sooner or later the hangman figured to bust his fool neck for him in any case. You and your sister were right. He really was a wicked son of a bitch."

Chapter 7

Thus it came to pass that Monday morning young Henry looked up from his typewriter to see Longarm looming in the doorway, looking disheveled, even for him. Henry smirked and said, "It's about time you got back to Denver. Where's your prisoner?"

"Dead and buried," Longarm said. "I caught him trying to escape up an Indian's ass. Then I had to ride for the nearest rail stop and— Never mind the tedious details, Henry. Is the boss in the back?"

Henry shook his head and said, "No. He's out looking for a lawyer for you. What got into you over to Stateline, you damned lunatic? Now we have two state governors as well as a U.S. senator yelling for your scalp!"

Longarm shrugged and said, "I can worry about that later. Now I want you to scout me up at least a dozen good deputies, old son. Have 'em mounted up and ready to ride when I get back from the county clerk's office, hear?"

Henry gasped, "What are you talking about? Ready to ride where, for Pete's sake?"

Longarm said, "I ain't after Pete. I'm after the last of the Bacon gang. I'll know better where to find 'em once I go through some county records. You go look for the backup I'll need."

He saw Henry hadn't leaped to his feet yet, so he added in a no-nonsense growl, "That's a direct order, *do* it!" before he spun on a heel and headed back downstairs.

His own McClellan saddle and a livery horse he didn't know as well were waiting near a side entrance of the federal building. Longarm mounted up and loped the brute toward the civic center to see if there was anything he ought to know about it before he did any serious riding. The old bay behaved all right, but a lot of city folk gawked rudely at them as they tore by. City folk were like that.

At the county hall of records Longarm found an old prune who struck him as the sort of cuss that Henry might turn into in his declining years if he didn't watch out. He told the old cuss his problem. The petty bureaucrat must have known Longarm didn't have the power to fire him or the lack of sense to hit him. For he sniffed as if he smelled sheep shit on Longarm's breath and said, "I don't see how our records would be of any service to you. There are thousands of property deeds on file, and you say you don't know anyone's name or even what part of the county you're talking about."

"I don't think you were listening," Longarm growled. "That gang member I just told you about was cagey about names. But he let more than one thing slip. He put his gang's hideout in the Front Range, and let slip it was a mineral claim. That eliminates a heap of pig farms and potato patches right off. We don't even have to consider clay pits if they're north, south, or east of town."

The musty old clerk shrugged and asked, "Have you any idea how many mining claims there are in the Front Range?"

Longarm nodded but said, "He never mentioned no mine. He said mineral claim. Since he was too dumb to know the difference on his own, he must have been repeating the words of his elders. Had it been a regular mine he'd have heard it called that. Denver is famous for its brick and pottery works. A lot of it's built and even paved with red sandstone. What'll you bet we're talking about a clay pit or brownstone quarry?"

The older man pursed his prunish lips and said, "I'm not a betting man. If I was I'd still have to pass. For there's clay almost anywhere you want to dig a few feet down, and those same red rocks crop out all along the first foothill ridges. How do you know your unfortunate prisoner wasn't talking about a gravel pit or fuller's earth, if you want to really cover all bets?"

Longarm swore softly and said, "Look, you do have all such claims on file, right?"

The fussbudget smugly replied, "We do, in no more than fifty drawers, in alphabetical order. Would you rather start with *A's* or *Z's?*"

Longarm said, "With my luck the name of the official owner fronting for the gang could start with an *M*. Let's try her yet another way. You do keep death certificates on file, right?"

The older man looked pained and said, "Vital statistics are filed separately. But naturally we file all birth, marriage, and death certificates. That's what we're here for."

"I was starting to wonder," Longarm said. "A year or so back the owners of that whatever gunned a man for trespassing, and they told the sheriff. Wouldn't there have to be a coroner's report and a county death certificate to go with that yarn?"

The older man displayed a flicker of interest in his watery oyster-gray eyes, but then he had to ask, "What was the dead man's name and when did he die?"

Longarm snorted in disgust and insisted, "Dammit, we ain't talking about a drunk run over by a streetcar or a kid dying of scarlet fever. Death by gunshot has to be a mite unusual, even in this county. Don't you keep natural and less natural deaths in separate files?"

The obstinate old bastard glanced at a wall clock, sighed, and said, "Wait here." Then he wandered off somewhere in the back and Longarm smoked two cheroots down to stubs before the man came back, looking even more dusty but sort of pleased with himself. Longarm was expecting some dusty but substantial records. He saw all the old jasper had for him was a slip of foolscap with a few lines penciled on it. But as he handed it over, the old fart said, "You were right. Less than a hundred white males have died of gunshot wounds in the past eighteen months, and you ought to be ashamed of yourself for shooting that many inside the county line, Deputy Long. Only one poor devil was shot as a trespasser in the hills to the west. His name was Davidson. I wrote it down for you."

Longarm said, "I know your files are precious to you, but do you mind if I look up just where he might have been trespassing when he got shot?"

The old man looked pained and asked, "What do you think I was doing back there all this time, jerking off? It's all down here, save the small print. Davidson was lawfully shot on property posted by the Amalgamated Building Stone Company. Jefferson County, by the way.

We wouldn't have had anything at all on file if the deceased hadn't been a Denver resident."

Longarm took the sheet of paper with a nod of thanks, but as he scanned it, he said, "That's odd. Big Bob told me the sheriff didn't raise much of a fuss because the dead man was just a saddle tramp, passing through."

The old clerk shrugged and said, "That's possible. Davidson's last known place of residence was a transient hotel on Larimer Street, and when I cross-checked for any local birth, school, or voter's registration, there wasn't any. He read like a sort of drifter who just happened to stay in Denver a spell before he poked about on someone else's property and wound up dead. You were right about it being a brownstone quarry, as you can see. Amalgamated is mostly owned by out-of-state stock holders. The little Jefferson County saw fit to offer us, along with a death certificate, is that the dead man was shot by the resident manager of the quarry, a man named Novak."

Longarm scanned the notes again, folded the paper, and put it away as he asked if there was a survey map handy that might show just where they were talking about. The older man shook his head and said, "Wrong county, if you're talking about large scale with property plats. You might try the county clerk over in Golden. They'd know better than us."

Longarm smiled thinly and said, "Come to study on it, I would like to check with Western Union in Golden about something else. I sure thank you, pard. You've been a great help."

The old prune-face said, "I know. Maybe someday you lawmen will get around to keeping your own copies of such records."

Longarm thanked him again, anyway, and tore back

101

out to mount up and ride back to the federal building. When he got there he found eight other deputies and half a dozen ponies waiting on the shady side of the street. He'd asked Henry to get him a dozen. He swore softly and said, "All right, boys, let's move it on out. Smiley, you and Dutch can't come unless you're up to running ten to fifteen miles afoot. Where did you figure I was headed when you failed to bring your ponies?"

Smiley said, "Henry never said. Does Billy Vail know?"

Longarm saw the six less-argumentative men were mounting up. So instead of arguing, he said, "Column of twos and follow me."

They did. Young Deputy Guilfoyle, a steady man in a fight that Longarm had worked with before, fell in on his left to ask where the hell they were going. Longarm said, "Golden, for openers. Then, with any luck, we figure to round up the last of the Bacon gang before this day is over."

Guilfoyle thought about that as the small posse clattered on down the street a block or more. Then he said, "I figured the boss didn't know. He'd never send seven men to shoot it out with the Bad Bacons."

"Would you like to be excused for the rest of the afternoon?" asked Longarm dryly.

Guilfoyle answered with a mean little grin of his own. "No thanks, teacher. I was on courtroom duty when Henry hauled me off all breathless. We heard what you done to the gang, solo, when there was more of 'em left. You say they're hid out in Golden?"

Longarm shook his head and replied, "No. Their last known address is. They've been hiding out in a posted quarry between jobs. I got the name of the place and the jasper running it for absentee owners. The county clerk in Golden will be able to pin her down better for us. I

102

doubt it can be too far from the county seat. A gang member called Stubby wired a pal named Johnson, care of the Golden telegraph office. I can see why he might be shy about home delivery. But how far would anyone want to ride in for important messages?"

As they rode on he filled his junior deputy in with all the details he knew. Guilfoyle proved he might just be overage in grade when he repeated that quarry manager's name a few times and said, "Bacon, backwards, would be Nocab, which just sounds dumb. I'd likely say it Novak by the time I'd played with it some."

Longarm said, "I follow your drift. Before Big Bob Bacon got too disgusting for me to string along further, he told me the outfit is a sort of outlaw clan, all related to one another by blood. Bacon is an old English name. Novak ain't."

Guilfoyle said, "Both names sound dumb, if you ask me. But didn't you say this Novak gent is only fronting for the gang, not riding out on jobs with 'em?"

Longarm nodded and replied, "All the more reason they'd want to know they could trust him. A man with no record of his own would be in a sweet spot to set 'em up for the considerable standing rewards on all their hides. I think you're right about him being a Bacon, backwards. Big Bob said they don't even marry up with gals they ain't close kin to."

Guilfoyle made a wry face and said, "I heard they was a sort of disgusting bunch. How do you reckon such a bunch of inbred half-wits ever lasted this long?"

Longarm answered flatly, "Not all of 'em could be half-wits. Many an inbred fighting dog turns out sly as well as ugly. Given their ingrained habit of trusting no outsiders, and given a good safe place to hole up between jobs, it's no mystery why they're still at large. I wouldn't have found out as much as I know about the secretive bastards if I hadn't met up with that one junior member of the tribe, who the tribe considered too dumb to do anything but hold their horses for 'em. I never laid eyes on the one called Stubby and—Now that's kind of odd, when you study on it."

Guilfoyle asked what he was talking about. So Longarm explained, "The late Cyrus Dove didn't work as an actual clansman of the Bad Bacons. Why would an outfit so distrustful of even distant cousins send an outside contractor after me?"

Guilfoyle suggested, "Maybe he was a Bacon on his momma's side, or any old side. You know how crooks fib about their I.D."

But Longarm shook his head and said, "Not Dove. His yellow sheets go back to his beating up a teacher as a schoolboy in a part of this great land the Bacons never haunted."

Guilfoyle shrugged and said, "Maybe somebody *else* sent him after you, then. It happens, you know."

Longarm worked on that until they were clattering over the Platte River bridge. Then he said, "I fail to see why Cousin Stubby would wire so sardonic a message if the Bacons weren't expecting more cheerful news about the way old Cyrus made out. Hold on. He wired that he'd told 'em so, about me. That could mean he admired hell out of me, or it could mean he'd been against a mere outsider, rep or no rep, involved in family business."

Guilfoyle suggested, "At least some of 'em could have been sort of pissed at you for foiling that train robbery on 'em. You'd made it too hot for 'em to hang around Stateline. Try her this way. Rules are made to be broken. So someone in the pack did hire Dove to do you and, when it didn't work, another who'd had his doubts couldn't resist crowing about how smart *he* was."

Longarm said he'd go with that, for now, and they were soon far enough out of town for him to call a trail break. As the seven of them watered the tumbleweeds along the side of the wagon trace, Longarm took time to light another smoke and give them all a quick rundown on where they were headed and why. From the way they all grinned, he was just as glad he'd had to leave old Smiley and Dutch behind. He wanted to take at least some of the gang alive for questioning, and it was hard to do that when Smiley and Dutch tagged along. Smiley had never smiled in human memory. It just happened to be his name. Dutch had been known to smile and even laugh, mostly after he'd gut-shot some owlhoot. Longarm told the men with him, "I know how much we all admire the Bad Bacons, boys. But remember, I'm in command, and I reckon Guilfoyle here can be my segundo when and if we get to surround that hideout. I want you all to wait for the command to open fire. There's said to be at least one woman shacked up in or near that quarry. There could be more. So I want 'em taken civilized, not Sand Creek style, hear?"

Not a few of them called him a durned old spoilsport. But they saddled up and rode on. Now that they were out on dirt instead of paving they got to ride faster. So by noon they rode into the mining town and county seat of Golden, and Longarm dismounted and strode into the Western Union office as the rest of the boys made for the saloon just across the way.

The clerk on duty was a motherly old gal, a lot more anxious to help than that pesky old clerk back in Denver. But all the help she could give him was that the message from Stateline to a Mr. Johnson had yet to be picked up.

Longarm frowned across the counter at her and said, "Now, that strikes me sort of odd, ma'am. We're talking about a telegram sent a couple of nights ago at the latest."

She said, "Don't blame Western Union for that, young man. Anyone can see it got here less than an hour after it was sent. Can we help it if people simply don't come in for wires addressed to them?"

He had to allow they couldn't. So he thanked her, left, and seeing he was walking already, strode just up the street to the county clerk's office.

This time he met a younger version of Henry. But, having fewer files to ride herd on, the jasper only took a few minutes to dig out the deed on the mysterious quarry and look its location up for Longarm on the Jefferson County survey map. He said he couldn't offer even the law a copy of the map, but that he'd be proud to trace the property lines on onionskin for Longarm. As he did so, casting an anxious eye at Longarm now and again, the taller deputy remembered his manners and said, "I ain't cussing under my breath at you. I'm cussing the cuss who seems to have slickered me."

Then Longarm took the penciled onionskin with more profuse thanks and strode catty-corner to the saloon, cussing most of the way. When Longarm joined his followers at the bar, Guilfoyle asked how come he seemed to be all glary-eyed at the moment. So Longarm said, "That goddamned quarry is down near Buffalo Creek."

Guilfoyle whistled morosely and said, "That's quite a ride. I don't see how we'll make her this side of sundown."

Longarm growled, "I just said that. We got to try. For even the one who calls his fool self Johnson seems to be forted up with the others in that quarry, and I can't see hitting 'em after dark, if they know we're coming."

Deputy Flynn, on the other side of him, asked,

"What makes you think they're expecting us?"

"They're acting like they do," Longarm said. "I don't know how they could have guessed who busted Big Bob out of the Stateline lockup, but, like I said, they can't all be stupid as he was."

It wasn't easy, even riding reckless, but they made it with a little less than an hour's worth of daylight to work with. They didn't ride up to the gate facing the wagon trace, of course. Using the improvised map, Longarm posted Guilfoyle with two of the boys near the road, albeit around a bend, out of sight from the ramshackle cluster of frame shacks just inside the gate. Then he took Flynn and two others with him up a steep draw as far as they could ride before he bade them dismount and follow him in the rest of the way afoot with their carbines. He carried his own Winchester one-handed, studying the onionskin held in the other. It called for some walking. The quarry property covered almost a full section, most of it steep as hell. When they worked themselves up to some second-growth aspen he led them through the cover, over the ridge between the route he'd chosen and the steep-walled valley the Amalgamated claim occupied. The fence along the crest of the ridge was six-stranded with a wooden sign on every other fence post. So they got to read, DANGER! HIGH EXPLOSIVES! NO TRESPASSING! SURVIVORS WILL BE PROSECUTED!

Flynn asked if Longarm wanted the fence cut or just pushed over. Longarm said, "Let's see if we can ease through it. I'd like to go easy on property damage until I find out whether the stockholders of this property know what else it's being used for."

So they all rolled under the bottom strand. Only one of them tore a sleeve enough to cuss about. On the far

107

side the aspen were thicker, with lots of fireweed and such, waist-high between the smooth gray-green aspen trunks. So it was easy enough for the four of them to spread out and move back toward the wagon trace, guns at port arms as they watched where they planted their boot heels going down the steep slope.

Longarm and everyone on his side froze when they heard a pony nicker through the trees ahead. Longarm took the lead, gliding between the trunks like an Indian's shadow, until he'd scouted the clearing ahead and waved the others down to join him.

There was a remuda of nine mounts grazing free of saddle or bridle in the four-odd acres of fenced-in grass, with a babbling brook running through it. He told his followers, "Big Bob said they all hid out up at this end when visitors came to call. So watch for a cabin or, hell, a roll of toilet paper, as we work around this clearing."

They did, without incident, at first. Then they ran out of cover. The grass and weeds they were standing on ended in a sheer sixty-foot drop. The valley stream to their right plunged over the same rim as a skinny waterfall down the red sandstone of the quarry that had been blasted out almost from fence line to fence line. The falling water formed a scummy green pond far below before winding on again as a muddier stream until it passed the five, no, six structures of unpainted, sun-silvered cedar. Longarm hunkered down near a clump of soapweed near the edge and said, "Well, the ponies we passed mean someone has to be home. We got 'em within tolerable long-gun range, so I reckon I'll just knock on the back door. The rest of you hold your fire 'til we see if they want to come sensible."

Suiting actions to words, Longarm sighted on the doorknob of the biggest shack and fired. He missed the knob, of course, but not by much, and so as the back door lost some paneling, folk inside tore out the front door, or tried to. Up on the quarry rim, Longarm and the deputies with him could only assume the joyous rebel yell that rose above the sound of the fusillade from Guilfoyle's party meant that at least one of the rascals had been hit.

There was a long sober silence. Then the back door opened just a crack and someone waved a white dish towel on the end of a rifle barrel.

Longarm called down, "That's not good enough, boys. If you want to come along quiet, toss your guns out ahead of you and then join 'em, hands as high as they'll go."

A hoarse and desperate voice called back to him, "Who are you and what do you mean by firing into an innocent business establishment? Can't you read? We got *dynamite* in here, you damned fools!"

Longarm called back, "You have the honor of addressing the U.S. Justice Department in all its glory. Stalling for sunset ain't going to work. I make it less than a quarter hour before nightfall, and the light's already getting tricky. So come on out while we can still see your innocent intent. To show you what a sport I am, you got, oh, two full minutes to make up your minds. Then I reckon we'll just do it the mean way."

There was no answer. Longarm figured they were arguing like hell inside. So he called out again, "I know you boys are stupid. But try to study on the edge we have on you. Them thin wood walls won't stop a pistol ball, and I have a mess of long-guns at my beck and call. By the way, your studying time's about up. I just hate to try and identify a dead man after dark."

The one near the door almost sobbed, "We need more time. Don't you dare shoot up these sheds! We got boxes and boxes of infernal dynamite in here!"

Longarm grimaced and said, "The last time they warned me it was nitro. I just can't abide a bullshit artist who never seems to change his story."

Then he raised his Winchester and proceeded to pump round after round of hot slugs into the establishment as, beside him, Flynn laughed above the roar of gunfire and proceeded to unload his own Winchester the more amusing way.

Then somebody got lucky—on Longarm's side, that is—and the resulting explosion was heard in Denver, according to later editions of the *Post*. Up closer, it was a lot more awesome. Longarm's hat flew off as he ducked down, and the whole quarry seemed to fill with one big fireball for quite a spell. Then splinters, planks, structural beams, and even a potbellied stove rained down forever from the monstrous anvil-headed thunder cloud that had not been blotting out the sunset so a few moments ago. As he raised his face from the grass, ears ringing and mouth gagging on sickly sweet nitro-glycerine fumes, Longarm spat out some grit and muttered, "Well, all right, maybe that time they were telling the truth."

Later, even with a bonfire of debris to shed light on the subject, all Longarm and his posse were able to gather together were fourteen guns that would never fire again, enough boot heels to account for eight and a half men, and a couple of more frenchified heels that added up to two different gals or one with a spare pair. None of these clues were gathered from the bare earth of the crater itself. The blast had dug a hole eight feet deep and two dozen across, razing if not vaporizing the entire site. It was Guilfoyle, naturally, who asked how they were going to convince the rest of the world they'd cleaned up the Bacon gang after wiping them from the face of this earth so entire.

Longarm shrugged and said, "We won't know 'til we see how many robberies they might or might not pull off after tonight. If we didn't get 'em all, we sure got eight or more of 'em. And that's about the numbers I had worked out. So let's put out that fire and carry what's left back to Denver, lest old Billy Vail worry about us being out so late."

They did. It was shorter, cutting catty-corner from the south end of Jefferson County across mostly open range, once they were downslope a mite. But it was still pushing midnight when they reined in at the livery near the federal building, and Longarm dismissed his detail for the night with congratulations on a job well done.

He was too bushed himself to consider climbing Capitol Hill just to get at a widow woman who'd likely be there, just as willing, tomorrow night. So he walked stiffly home to his hired digs on the unfashionable side of Cherry Creek, and with some effort, and not a little temptation to just flop across the bed and to hell with it, undressed and climbed in more civilized.

But it seemed he'd no sooner gotten to sleep when some damn fool was pounding on his chamber door. It didn't sound like a raven. It was getting sort of light outside, dammit. So he got up, went to the door naked but armed, and moaned, "Who's there and how come? Can't you see it's the middle of the infernal night?"

It was Henry from the office. Since he was either having an asthma attack out in the hall or something worse, Longarm let him in, and, sure enough, it was worse.

"Longarm, you're really in trouble, now." Henry sort of wheezed, explaining, "I ran all the way. Marshal Vail said to."

Longarm said, "I never said you were panting for my fair white body, Henry. What else could have you and old Billy so gaspy at this hour?"

"You," Henry said. "Whatever possessed you to destroy the Amalgamated Building Stone Company with all that dynamite?"

Longarm said, "Hell, I never destroyed it. I just made the quarry a mite deeper. As to why I did it, it was infested with crooks. The Bad Bacons, to be exact."

Henry shook his head wildly and said, "So you say. The boss has already had Guilfoyle and Flynn on the carpet. There's not a shred of evidence that anyone named Bacon was ever anywhere near that property. So all we can be sure of is that you just about destroyed the same, along with let's hope no more than a few employees. Don't you know who owned at least half the stock in that outfit, Longarm?"

A fuzzy ball of fur woke up in Longarm's stomach as he asked soberly, "Somebody more important than anyone named Bacon?"

Henry said, "More important than Marshal Vail or even the state governor he's pals with. You just blew the considerable shit out of Senator Winger's brownstone quarry!"

Chapter 8

Billy Vail was too short to actually lead Longarm down the hall by one ear. But the effect was much the same as the irate Marshal hauled him into a seldom-used spare office, telling him to shut up, sit down, and speak when he was spoken to.

Inside, a severely pretty brunette sat severely at a conference table in a severe black suit with a pad of ruled yellow paper and a sheaf of freshly sharpened pencils in front of her, obviously raring to go.

Vail shoved Longarm down at a bentwood chair across from the gal, saying, "Miss Amanda, this is the troubled youth I told you about. Longarm, this is Amanda Bleeker, Esquiress, the only lawyer I could get at such short notice who was willing to even talk to you. I'll be in my own office if either of you lets out a cry for help."

As Vail grumped out, the lady across the table smiled in a frosty way and told Longarm, "I'm not a member of the good-old-boys' bar, actually. When I graduated from law school I had the choice of waiting on tables or working for the Justice Department as a legal secretary. Fortunately, anyone can act as your legal advisor during a congressional inquiry, and Marshal Vail may manage to recruit a more imposing defense team for you by the time they actually indict you."

Longarm took off his hat and planted it to one side on the big table between them as he said, just as firmly, "Hold on, ma'am. You're confusing me a mite, no offense. For like I just tried to tell Billy Vail, I ain't the one who needs a lawyer. Old Windy Winger is the one who needs a lawyer. We got him nailed in the box as a confederate, if not the leader, of an owlhoot gang!"

She shushed him with a severe look, glanced down at the notes she'd written so far, and said, "Item One: On the last day of last month Senator Howard Winger announced he was forming a special committee to investigate charges that federal marshals and their deputies were exceeding their authority as vested in them by Congress in many states and territories out this way. Less than a week after that was published in the local papers you, Deputy Marshal Custis Long, shot the senator's personal bodyguard, John Henry Calhoun, pleading self-defense.'"

"That's what it was," said Longarm. "He was after me. I don't recall reading anything about no congressional anything in the *Post*. I generally skip political items to save needless wear and tear on my faith in humanity."

She said, "I believe you. They're going to point out that it was printed on the front page and that your personnel records indicate you can read. But shall we go on? Item Two: On a routine mission to pick up and transport a federal prisoner, you locked three men in a boxcar and smoked them to death."

Longarm snorted in disbelief and said, "It was a mail car, and the poor innocent victims were robbing it after

114

gunning two men before I could stop 'em. Didn't the Pinkertons take the credit for smoking them Bacons?"

"Apparently not," she said, "once they found out there was to be a congressional inquiry into such brutal punishments in the name of the law. Senator Winger is on record as an opponent of the death penalty, even *after* a proper trial and conviction."

Longarm grimaced and said, "I can see why he'd just about have to be. Can't you get it through your pretty little head that me and the boys just proved the two-faced rascal was aiding and abetting a gang wanted for mad-dog rampaging?"

She sniffed and said, "We'll get to *that* charge against you in a minute. As for the crack about my pretty little head, would that mean you share the usual views of your muscular gender on the subject of women taking part in the legal profession?"

He shook his head and said, "No, ma'am, I hate all lawyers, regardless of religion, color, or sex. Conversations such as this one only tend to confirm how unprejudiced I am. Why in thunder are we talking about nit-picky charges against me when we ought to be swearing out a warrant on that infernal Senator Winger?"

She said, "Marshal Vail asked the same question until we went over the brief against you. Both Kansas and the state of Colorado charge you with aiding and abetting the escape of one Robert 'Big Bob' Bacon. Fortunately, *they* can't have you until Senator Winger's committee gets through with you."

He smiled sheepishly and said, "Aw, I'd have no doubt won that jurisdictional dispute had I hung around Stateline long enough. I just saved everyone a lot of needless argument and, better yet, got Big Bob to tell us about that hideout on old Winger's property, see?"

She made a note, but shook her head and said, "Robert Bacon didn't tell *us* a thing. You failed to bring him back to Denver as you were ordered to. Marshal Vail says you . . . murdered and buried him out on the prairie?"

Longarm said, "Hold on. It wasn't quite that informal. I had to kill him for . . . acting unruly. I saw no need to carry him all the way back in high summer. Billy's taken my word on crooks we no longer have to worry about many a similar time."

The brunette wrinkled her nose and murmured, "That's another thing the committee will no doubt want to ask about. How are we going to explain blowing up Amalgamated Building Stone and anyone who might have been working there?"

He laughed incredulously and said, "Hell, ask the boys who rode after the Bad Bacons with me!"

"We did. You'll be pleased to know they all seem to think they were after the Bacon gang, too. But after that it just won't wash. You and your posse were the aggressors, on posted property. The people working on or guarding the property had the right to open fire on you, first, but they didn't. You, Custis Long, fired the first shot. Whether you knew there were high explosives to worry about or not, you kept firing until the place was blown to kingdom come."

He nodded and said, "Sure we did. Make that, sure *I* did, since I was in command. I gave the gang the chance to surrender peacefully. They chose not to. So I got 'em as best I could."

She asked bluntly, "How do we go about proving that? Is there any way to identify one body as a wanted criminal? Senator Winger says he'd left a couple called Novak in charge up there and that he never heard of anyone named Bacon."

Longarm started to say something, swallowed it as useless, and said instead, "I've heard of raw, but that rascal don't even crack 'em out of the rotten eggs to rub a man's nose in! Can't you see what he's trying to get away with?"

She nodded and said, "I'm on your side. Marshal Vail said I had to be. But I have to say it reads more than one way to me, and the others on that committee will be personal pals of old Windy Winger. The chairman of a committee hardly ever selects *enemies* to sit with him. I'm going to start by asking him to disqualify himself, since he's the one who seems to feel you have some personal grudge against him."

Then she shot him a keen look and asked, "*Do* you have some personal grudge against him, ah, Custis?"

Longarm shook his head but said, "I do *now*. But I never when *he* commenced sending hired guns after *me*. I wouldn't know him right now if I woke up in bed with him!"

She hesitated. Then she asked, "What about waking up in bed with his wife? I understand Regina Winger is attractive and, ah, you do have a reputation as a sort of rustic Romeo, according to the girls down the hall in the typing pool."

He shrugged modestly and said, "That's sure a good reason not to mess with the gals where you work. But as for the Senator's woman, I've never met her, neither. Don't they spend most of their time in Washington these days?"

Amanda nodded and said, "That's where she is right now. But, like her husband, she hails from Colorado, and some say she was sort of wild in her youth."

He said, "So was I. Are you asking if I was ever wild with her before she might have married up with his nibs?"

117

Amanda nodded some more and pointed out, "A thing like that could make even a younger and better-looking husband send a hired gun after someone. That's taking your word it was Calhoun after you and not vice versa. They say the senator hired his so-called body-guards to keep an eye on his wife, not him. He likes to assure one and all that he packs two guns and can take care of himself."

Longarm thought before he answered, "There wasn't any ladies present when I had it out with Calhoun be-hind the city hall. How long has Windy Winger been married up with such a guarded condition, ma'am?"

She looked at her notes. He was glad she wasn't given to guessing games as she replied, "They've been married nine years. No children. I see she's careful about her body, too. Why do you ask, if you say you don't know her?"

He heaved a sigh of relief and said, "I wanted to be sure I don't know her. I met lots of wild gals when I first came to Denver, six or eight years ago. But I never mess with married women, even when they ain't body-guarded. But, for the record, do you have exactly what she looks like in them notes?"

The frosty brunette made a wry face and said, "No, but I've had her pointed out to me at more than one reception. When they come west to campaign they both get the red-carpet treatment. I recall her as a brassy blonde of forty or so. To give her credit for all the effort she must put into it, she does manage to look younger. She tries to put on the airs of a gracious society woman. But the apple never falls far from the tree and, while one can take a girl out of a mining-camp shack, you can't take the mining-camp shack out of the girl. I imagine most men would be fooled by her. But another woman can always spot bad breeding and piggy private habits."

Longarm shrugged and said, "There you go. I'd surely recall a bodyguarded pig. The more I study on it the more I feel her husband had more sensible reasons for starting up with me. He knew one member of the Bacon gang was being held, federal, over to Stateline. He knew Billy Vail would surely send a deputy over yonder to pick him up and carry him back here to Denver, just as his uncle, cousin, or whatever was fixing to get elected some more by getting written up in the local papers. He knew how dumb Big Bob could be. So he didn't want me anywhere near him and—"

"It won't work," she cut in. "You hadn't been ordered to pick the prisoner up, as yet, when that unfortunate Calhoun picked a fight with you, or vice versa."

Longarm scowled and said, "There was vice but no versa in the cards, ma'am. In all modesty, I'm better known for slickering crooks than seducing stenographers. They didn't have to be *sure* I was the deputy Billy figured on sending after Big Bob. They only had to *worry* about it being me. Had Calhoun won, and it was close, Billy would have had to send somebody else, and most of the boys transport prisoners more routine. The gang might have been sort of laying for the train meant to bring Big Bob *back*. Only, being mad-dog stupid as well as having the time on his hands, Nasty Nate decided they may as well rob that train as long as they were out there anyway. Of course, when things went not at all the way they'd planned, they had to just run for it, back to that quarry, and—"

"That's enough," she cut in, explaining, "you don't have to convince me you got a prisoner you can't produce to tell you how to find where the others you can't produce might have been hiding. You have to convince a congressional committee that you haven't made up the whole story out of thin air to justify picking on their own dear committee chairman and, dammit, you can't even produce a *scalp* that you can connect with any wanted outlaw!"

He stared at her soberly and tried, "Would the dead train robbers or old Big Bob help?"

She shook her head and told him, "Not unless they could sit up and sign some depositions backing your story. I don't expect Senator Winger to press us too hard on outlaws you had some possible *reason* to brutalize, as he likes to put it. The sticky point is that we just can't prove a word the late Robert Bacon might have said to you, and you alone, before you rightly or wrongly killed him. That leaves it your word and yours alone that you had just cause to suspect anyone remotely connected to the Bacon gang was on the premises when you blew any and everybody who *was* there to teeny weeny bits!"

He started to reach for a cheroot, decided she already seemed disgusted enough with him, and soberly said, "Well, maybe we can plead a total lack of corpus delicti and offer to pay for property damages. Teeny weeny works both ways, right?"

She said, "Wrong. Corpus delicti means the body of the crime, whether there's a human corpse to go with it or not. Your own friends would have to testify, under oath, that somebody was in at least one of those shacks when you blew them all to match sticks. But let's not put the cart before the horse, Custis. You won't have to defend yourself in a regular court until the senator and his pals get all the political news coverage they can out of their public hearings."

He frowned and asked, "Ain't a congressional committee hearing the same as a trial?"

She repressed a shudder and told him, "Good

120

heavens, no. For one thing, rules of evidence and the right to cross examination apply in a regular court of law. By hauling you before a so-called-fact-finding committee, the old windbag gets to flay you alive in the public eye without any worries about your constitutional rights. They don't call him Windy Winger because he's logical and soft-spoken. I mean to object to as many foolish questions and accusations as I can, of course. But there's really no way to make them stick to the rules of legal procedure or even the subject of their investigation. I attended a hearing one time where, for no reason I or anyone else could see, a congressman insisted on reading *Uncle Tom's Cabin,* all of it, into the record."

Longarm scowled and said, "I don't care what the rascals want to read to me, Miss Amanda. The question is what can they *do* to me, if it ain't a proper trial?"

She sighed and said, "They can blacken you with tar we can't throw back at them. Such hearings tend to be fishing expeditions as well. They can ask questions and make accusations they'd never be able to under regular trial proceedings and, while their final committee report doesn't even give you the right to sue for slander, a lot of it will be printed in the papers, long before we *do* get hauled into court by the ambitious prosecution that's sure to follow the committee's bad report on you. Then where are we to select a jury that hasn't already read what a no-good rascal you must be, to have all those fine political sages so mad at you already?"

Longarm whistled softly and said, "All in all, I'd rather start out with a judge and jury and take my chances. How soon do you figure I'll get hauled before Windy Winger and his panel of pet kangaroos, Miss Amanda?"

"How do you feel about this time tomorrow morning at the opera house, on stage?" she asked.

"Awful," he said. "I might have known they'd want to play to a bigger audience then we could jam in any regular courtroom in town. But if that's what they want, I'll just have to be there with bells on."

But as he got to his feet with a resigned smile, she asked him where on earth he thought he was going, adding, "We have to prepare your defense. Sit down."

He didn't. He said, "You've already told me I got to sit on stage at the opera house like a snowball in hell getting laughed at, Miss Amanda. As I see it, the best defense is an offense. I know Senator Winger is trying to cover up for his kin, the Bacon bunch, by abusing his powers even worse than most politicians feel safe. He knows I know who's guilty and who ain't around here. But he figures I can't prove it and, right now, I can't. So I got maybe twenty-four hours to come up with some proof, and, no offense, I suspect even my own lawyer suspects I'm a sort of homicidal maniac, even if she's too polite to say so."

His legal advisor looked down at the table between them as she murmured, "Marshal Vail assured me half the things they say about you are just not true. I really need more notes before we appear before that committee, Custis."

He said, "I'll scout you up later if I don't come up with anything better than my word against a political polecat's. But right now, with your leave, I got to go polecat hunting."

Chapter 9

Smiley and Dutch caught up with Longarm as he passed the Parthenon Saloon. Smiley was a tall, morose-looking breed, even when he wasn't pissed off. The shorter and paler Dutch always seemed cheerful, unless you looked into his ice-cold eyes of gunmetal blue-gray. As they fell in on either side of Longarm, Dutch said, "I hope we're on our way to visit old Windy Winger, pard. They say he keeps a hunting pack of hired guns, and business has been slow around here of late."

Longarm said, "I ain't stalking him just yet. I don't want you boys stalking him either. How would it look if a big shot from Washington got shot the day before he was to hold himself a hearing on how brutal us boys might be?"

On his other side, Smiley growled, "A lot less complicated, for openers. Can't we even run the rascal out of town for you? We could do it without killing him all the way, given a bucket of hot tar and some feathers."

Longarm shook his head and said, "I want to nail him right or not at all. He's already opined in print that

123

our more western ways of dealing with crooks tend to be uncouth."

Dutch insisted, "Dammit, Longarm, we just talked to Guilfoyle and some of the other boys. That windy old son of a bitch is loco as the rest of the Bacons if he thinks he can bully real men in such a sissy way!"

Longarm said, "Uncle Sam ain't no sissy. He pays our wages, and unless or until I can prove different, Uncle Sam is backing Senator Winger's play. I'm headed for the press room of the *Post* to talk to another old pal about how close the bastard could be related to the Bacon clan. If you boys really want to help, you could find out something else for me. I can't be everywhere at once, and they'll let you boys at any files they might let me at."

Dutch moaned and said, "Oh, shit, not paperwork. I'd rather herd cows."

But Smiley said, *"Any* chore has herding cows beat. What are we after, pard?"

Longarm said, "I'm accused of gunning one and only one hired gun on Winger's payroll. Not a word on Cyrus Dove, who came after me in Stateline on a mighty similar mission. I'd like to know if that was just oversight on the senator's part, or whether Dove wasn't working for him official. Dove was packing a bounty hunter's license, Colorado, for all the good it did him. They might know over to the state license bureau who he said he was working for when he applied to them. You got to say you own or work for a private detective agency when you fill out the form. If I could prove I tangled with two men on Winger's payroll, one of whom followed me all the way to Stateline so's I could attack him, the senator might have as much fun explaining that as I would."

Dutch muttered about climbing the hill to the state

124

house. But Smiley, who always talked less and thus made more sense as a rule, said, "Consider it done. Whether Dove was on the official payroll or not, he was wanted in other parts. To get that license without a background check he'd have had to be vouched for by someone important as well as local. So that ought to be on file as well. If it ain't, we'll assume someone at the license bureau is on the take again, despite what Billy Vail did to that last bunch as a courtesy to his pal, the governor."

Longarm warned them to be gentle and added, "While you're at it, see if Cousin Stubby—No, forget it. Nobody would call himself Stubby on a license application. I'll see you boys this afternoon. Usual saloon after quitting time?"

Dutch said, "Shoot, I like the ambience of the Parthenon off duty or on." So they shook on it and parted friendly.

When he got to the *Post*, his best pal, Reporter Crawford, was out covering a suicide or murder at the Silver Dollar. It was hard to tell when a whore went out a window. Another reporter Longarm knew at least to jaw with said he'd be proud to help if there was anything he could do. So Longarm told him what he was after and the two of them ambled back to the morgue.

Newspaper morgues didn't smell quite as bad as the other kind, but the one at the *Post* made up for it by being hot and dusty as the two of them pawed through the files. The man who worked there was good at finding cross-references and, better yet, they had a whole mess of stuff on Senator Winger in one manila folder, seeing he kept running for reelection in Colorado when he wasn't pestering folk back east in Washington. There were even some photograph prints among the clippings from the *Post* and its many rival papers. The senator was a fiend for getting himself in the papers.

The friendly reporter identified a close-up sepia-tone portrait as that of the old boy himself. Smiling up off the brown paper so good-naturedly, Howard B. Winger didn't look like the devil incarnate, or even as two-faced as a lot of political hacks Longarm recalled. Of course, few of them could have had half as much practice at being two-faced, even running for public office. The old bastard had bushy black brows to go with his white, or in this case, light-brown hair. It was an easy face to remember. Longarm was sure he'd never had a fight or even a serious fuss with the cuss.

Another photo showed the same cuss full-length, in an outfit he might have stolen off the corpse of Abe Lincoln, standing with a nice-looking gal in a bridal gown. Longarm had never had a fuss with that face, either, albeit it might have been more fun. He asked the reporter next to him, "Bride or daughter?"

The more knowledgable reporter replied, "The old fart's wife. They have no kids. I think she looks too young for him, too. But you know how some gals are about wealth and power."

The reporter dug another picture out, saying, "Here's the old fart in a Sioux warbonnet. We'd sure like to run it. The *Post* is against him for a lot of better reasons. But we're waiting for them to get the kinks out of the Ben Day process before we try printing halftone on newsprint. Meanwhile we can only save such stuff and hope he never gets elected president. Our boss wants us to run the one with the warbonnet the day he does."

Longarm chuckled wryly and said, "I wouldn't, if I was opposed to him, political. Voters out this way are devoted to cowboys and Indians, and he seems to be trying to cover both grounds. Is there anything to this clipping, accusing him of winning the Battle of Cold Harbor, single-handed?"

The newspaper man said, "Naw, the Colorado Militia never got to fight that far east. Some say he rode with Chivington at Sand Creek that time. But he denies it. I'd deny it, too, if I was running for office from Colorado. Nobody but Chivington ever thought much of that idea."

Longarm said, "Not everyone in this state is a total fool. How would I go about tying Windy Winger into that sad affair if I really wanted to, before election time?"

The reporter whistled softly and said, "Hey, that's *my* story, if it's a story. We'd love to have something as nasty as *that* to hang on Windy Winger!"

He moved down the row of dusty files as Longarm went on thumbing through the biographical bull they had on his self-appointed enemy. Big Bob Bacon had told him the criminal clan he sprang from had festered in New York state for a spell before following the wagons west no earlier than the late forties. Senator Winger, blast his parents for being married proper, had been born in Pennsylvania in 1832, allowing him to come west and do all sorts of wonders after the Bacons were already out here. Longarm wasn't interested in all the Indians and Johnny Rebs a man who seemed to be against the death penalty had killed, in person, with cavalry sabers as well as guns, to hear him brag. He found a society page clipping on the old fart's younger wife to see if it might say who *she* could be related to. Both the widow woman on Sherman Avenue and Miss Amanda Bleeker were right about her pushing forty, albeit from the bottom. Allowing for a few years worth of fibbing, Regina Winger, nee Masterson, had been born in Baltimore and came west with her Pikes-Peak-or-bust parents, who hadn't really done so dramatic either way. The column, even trying to flatter her, had to settle for graduating her from the Evans Grammar School with the twelve-year-old class of 1854. He knew the big red sandstone school. He hadn't known it was that old. Back in '54 they'd have still been calling Denver Cherry Creek.

The reporter rejoined him, saying, "Colonel John Chivington, the fighting parson, moved back to Ohio after both the Colorado Volunteers and the Methodist Church said they wanted no more to do with such a baby-butchering cuss. We don't have his present address. I wouldn't want anyone from Colorado looking me up if I were him, either. But let's see, the state militia might still have a roster of all those dashing cavaliers who fought for the Union by slaughtering Indians. What year was Sand Creek, sixty-three?"

Longarm said, "Sixty-four. It's worth a try. But I don't know, a lot of such records seem to have been lost since the war. Political appointees who may have deserted in time of war just don't want gents like you and me looking up their service records. It can make my job a chore."

He held up the society page clipping and said, "I may have found a handier skeleton in the Winger family closet. The lady our famous hero married claims to be a graduate of a school that couldn't have been there before Denver was incorporated as a town in 1859. So where could she have gone to school, in a tent?"

The reporter took the clipping, scanned it, and said, "There could have been someone giving lessons in the three R's, back in our Cherry Creek days. But it's just as likely she was ashamed to tell the society editor she'd never been to school at all. Do you suspect her of something more serious?"

Longarm helped himself to another look at the pretty albeit not-too-bright-looking face under the bridal veil before he said, "Baltimore would know better. If she was born there like she says she was, within a few years either way, they ought to be willing to vouch for her. Just let me write down— Hell, it don't say who her parents might have been. All right, Regina Masterson on any birth certificate they have on file will have to do. I'd best go wire them. I'm sure obliged for such leads as you've just given me, pard."

The reporter said, "Jake. Jake Brown. You may have put me on to something about Senator Winger as well. I guess you know how the *Post* means to cover those hearings at the opera house, eh?"

Longarm hadn't thought about that. He said, "It just ain't true that I blow things up for spite. So you only have to print the truth."

They shook on it and he turned to go as the reporter began to put everything away. But then he turned to ask, "Say, if you wanted to ask questions about the ownership of a stone quarry, without going back up to Golden, how would you go about it? I didn't see anything about it in the senator's dossier. He just brags about owning all sorts of mines and cattle spreads, without giving any details."

The reporter took out a business card, wrote a name on the back of it, and said, "Carry this over to Sam Killbride at the brokerage firm of Feldman and Killbride, on Wynkoop, near the Union Depot. If anyone in this state is making a nickel on mineral rights, old Sam is sure to be interested."

Longarm put the card away with another nod of thanks and left.

He stopped at the first telegraph office he came to and sent his wire to Baltimore, spending an extra two bits of his own money to ask them to rush. Then he headed for the brokerage firm further downtown. But, crossing Larimer, it occurred to him he hadn't even eaten breakfast and here it was going on noon. So he stopped for chili con carne with fried eggs on top and, since he was in a hurry, only had one thick slice of minced pie with his third mug of coffee.

Sam Killbride turned out to be a friendly old gent with a good firm handshake for such a skinny gray cuss. He sat Longarm down in a back office, near a rolltop desk, and offered him a cigar. It smelled a lot better than the ones Billy Vail smoked, so he took it and struck a match for the both of them.

The older man heard him out, puffing quietly, and as he wound down, Longarm feared a well-meaning newspaperman had sent him on a snipe hunt. But then Killbride said, "I know that quarry. You did Windy Winger a favor with his insurance company by razing the site. It was about played out when he bought it, oh, let's see, three or four years ago. Brownstone houses are still in fashion, but only if you build 'em with top-grade stone. Aside from all the cracks running through the rock face up yonder, you might have noticed they've cut in about as deep as practical."

Longarm said, "I did notice the pit rose sort of high on my side, Sam. That's how come I chose to shoot instead of leap at that back door."

The older man nodded and said, "Building stone doesn't pay unless you can get it to town easy. The original owners never got much more than paving slabs off that mountain, by wagon. Old Winger was a fool to buy in when they reorganized as a public corporation. We were offered the deal. That's how come I know as much about it as I do. We wouldn't touch it. It struck us as no more than a scheme to

130

sell worthless stock without actually winding up in jail. They say Winger bought a controlling interest cheap enough, if we're talking money, and way the hell overpriced if we're talking real business."

"He may have had other reasons," Longarm said. "Am I correct in assuming a major stock holder could just about run such a losing proposition as he might choose to?"

Killbride nodded and said, "If you call letting property lay idle and paying taxes on it *running* it. I understand there is, or was, a caretaker and a handful of part-time quarry hands up there. Nobody ever suspected them of being anything else."

Longarm said, "Nobody was supposed to. Senator Winger claims to be a slick Colorado businessman when he ain't in Washington at monkey business. So, speaking purely as a businessman, Sam, would you say it made business sense to keep a worthless business fenced and maintained by anyone, at gunpoint?"

Killbride shook his head and said, "We heard about that poor drifter they gunned as a trespasser that time. They could have saved the ammunition by just letting him poke about and be on his way. There was nothing of value on the property. You just don't find anything in sandstone worth more than the stone itself, when it's halfway solid. Your notion of outlaws using it as a hideout works better than anything else I can dream up. But, to be fair, old Windy never visited the site. He hired a watchman as cheap as such help comes and likely forgot all about it."

Longarm shook his head and asked, "Don't even senators have to pay taxes on land they own personal. He'd get billed at least one time a year for that land, even if he kept the taxes on it up. I just don't see how a man could forget he was paying bills for even a few years, can you?"

Killbride frowned thoughtfully at the tip of his own cigar as he mused, "Well, old Windy is sort of busy as well as dumb. I can see one of his staff opening a bill from the Colorado tax collector, and just paying it along with all the other such annoyances. He does own other holdings, and brags on all of them, so—"

"I wish you hadn't said that," Longarm cut in with a weary sigh. "Even if I try to hook him that way, you just showed me how he'd be able to wiggle off. All he'd have to admit to is that, sure, he owned that quarry, but he'd forgot all about it until I blew every shred of more sinister business to shreds for him. Am I right in assuming the tax bill on that worthless section of mighty steep wouldn't come to all that much?"

The older man nodded soberly and said, "Maybe a nickel or so an acre for not only unimproved but disimproved marginal range. I follow your drift. I'm a more prudent man when it comes to paying bills, but we're no doubt talking less than his wife spends on her hairdresser in a year. I'd say you were wasting time baiting that hook, son. Like you just said, not one shred of evidence. Your only hope of making him look dumber than he's out to make you look would be to get something more solid than sloppy business methods on him. Most of the gents who vote for him so regular *admire* free-and-easy ways with money."

He put his cigar back between his teeth and almost growled, "Damn few of the fools ever had money to worry about. That's why they just love it when he raves on about free silver and damming all the creeks in the Front Range. Dam foolishness, if you ask a taxpayer. But the founding fathers slipped up on that point. Bread and circuses brought the Roman republic down, too.

Just you wait. Sooner or later they'll elect an idiot like Windy Winger to the oval office and *then* we'll be in for it!"

Longarm hadn't come to argue politics, so he excused himself as gracefully as he could manage and left to get back on the trail. He just hated paper trailing. But sometimes it was the only trail folks left when they spent most of their time in big towns like Washington and Denver. He couldn't get at anything on file in Washington, of course, but since Regina Winger had spent most of her life in and about Denver and her husband had been out this way a good twenty years, save a mysterious gap he tried to account for by bragging he'd been with the Colorado Volunteers between '63 and '65, despite said state militia's lack of documentation, neither of 'em seemed to have any past worth killing for.

By the time he'd worn out his legs and sweated up his collar beyond repair, Longarm had fleshed out the faded photographs with mental images of a man and wife no better, but not much worse, than most of the population still at large. Senator Winger added up to a fast-talking self-made man who'd left the usual trail of lawsuits and unpaid bills in his wake. He'd bounced more checks earlier in his career, before he'd made a few slick moves in mining and cattle. By the time he'd gotten into politics, more recent, he'd cleaned up his casual habits with other gents' money and, despite all the mean things the *Post* called him, didn't seem to be any more or less crooked than your average political big shot. If Longarm hadn't known better, he'd have had to give the son of a bitch a passing grade in integrity. When he wasn't making loud and senseless stump speeches, the old fart's voting record was surprisingly self-sacrificing. For despite the views of the cattle and mining interest he depended on for backing, he had some surprising views of his own, for a good old Colorado boy.

As he hung more paper flesh on the senator's wife, Longarm began to suspect the senator owed some of his less-ferocious side to the gal he'd married up with. For even Regina Winger's lies seemed well intended or at least understandable. At the Denver Board of Education they verified Longarm's doubts about a lady graduating from a school before it had been built. But later, as a grown woman, Regina Winger had indeed attended night school for illiterate adults and, better yet, after she'd learned to read and write, she'd taken part in all sorts of volunteer work for them. So Longarm had to forgive her for that white lie when a society reporter had caught her off guard with that question about her education. It was sort of pathetic to brag on graduating from a public grammar school. But to a gal who'd never gone to school at all, it had likely sounded high-toned enough.

The infernal old prune at the Hall of Records, who was no doubt getting tired of Longarm as well by now, verified that old Regina's parents had both died unmysterious in Denver, after she'd been old enough to look after herself, and neither death certificate mentioned anyone named Bacon as possible kin. The mother had been a Norris who'd croaked of the cholera just about the time the Denver Board of Health was making folk fill in their homegrown wells between Cherry Creek and the South Platte, neither being fit to drink from. The late Zeke Masterson had lasted long enough to strike color one summer in the Front Range. It hadn't amounted to all that much. But he had left his only child, Regina, enough to get by on for a few years, and before it had run out she'd met and married Howard Winger, taught him some manners, and likely persuaded him to go into politics. That's what men with a bullying streak tended to do; once they got too old to fight physical, they went into politics so they could bully poor, hard-working U.S. deputies.

Neither the senator nor his younger wife had been spring chickens when they married up. Even the gal had been running for old maid when she finally hooked the rich old cuss. That put some bees in Longarm's Stetson. But try as he might, he just couldn't connect Winger's late-blooming bride to any whorehouse or previous husband. If the gal had made friends with any other woman's husband in her protracted spinsterhood, it had never made the police blotters or divorce courts. Longarm decided thirty-odd-year-old virgins were at least possible and, if she'd made up for a deprived youth once she'd wed the uncouth Windy Winger, that could account for the hold she had to have on him.

He could tell she did when he matched up her social work and regular church going and charity doings with the fits and starts of sissy legislation the senator kept upsetting some of his back-home backers with. Trying to abolish hanging was astounding enough. But from time to time he'd come up with notions like outlawing personal side arms, easy money, and even a tax on personal income! It was small wonder the dumb bastard was trying to get back on the front pages of his home-state newspapers with another election coming up. Attacking the law in a part of the country that didn't have enough law to begin with was hardly the way Longarm would have done it. But, then, he wasn't running for reelection with a self-made society lady filling his head with all sorts of goody-two-shoes notions. Longarm was glad the infernal woman had gone back to Washington to pick the birdies and feed the roses in their town-house garden. Without her egging him on, old Windy Winger might make more sense at that hearing.

Near sundown, in the Parthenon, Longarm found Smiley and Dutch had beaten him there by at least two drinks. As Longarm bellied up to the bar with the boys, Dutch said, "You was right on the money about Cyrus Dove getting his bounty hunting permit with a letter from a U.S. senator. But after that it falls apart."

Longarm tried to signal the barkeep and cock an eyebrow at Dutch at the same time. It was Smiley who volunteered, "They told us Dove's license had been revoked. Seems the senator's wife, Miss Regina, fired him personal for fibbing about his background. She swore out a warrant regarding some missing silver as well. Cyrus Dove was sailing under false colors when he came after you in Stateline the other night."

Longarm got his schooner and sipped some suds as he thought that over. Then he mused aloud, "The man who hired him in the first place might not have been as fussy as his wife. But I just can't see asking him, in front of witnesses, why he might have wanted to hire a gent with a record."

Dutch reached in a vest pocket, saying, "He hired six, all told. I wrote down all the names here, including the two you've already shot. All of them put down on their applications that they needed private detective permits to act as personal bodyguards of the senator and his lady. What I can't figure out is why a couple who spends most of their time back east would recruit a private honor guard *out west*."

Longarm said, "That's easy. Since John Wilkes Booth acted so dramatic at Ford's Theatre, the Secret Service keeps a sharp eye on even rent receipts in the District of Columbia. I'd just hate to apply for any sort of license there if I had a thing to hide. On the other

136

hand, a Colorado permit to guard a senator from Colorado ought to get one by, should any D.C. copper badge inquire about a bulged-out frock coat and no other visible means of support, late at night."

He took the slip from Dutch with a nod of thanks and tucked it into his own vest, saying, "I'll worry about the four left, later. I've about walked my fool feet off and anything on file about 'em will be locked up for the night by now."

Smiley growled, "Give us credit for knowing our trade. We already scouted for 'em. I got Dutch here to promise he'd let me take 'em alive. Only they ain't in town."

Dutch added wistfully, "The senator must think he's tougher than his old woman. He's guarded by no more than a snooty room clerk and the house dick at the Majestic Hotel, along with them other dudes from Washington. He sent all four of their hired guns east with old Regina. They guard her forty-year-old body like she was at least a grand duchess. We talked to some railroad gents at the Union Depot about it. They say she rode both ways in high style, in her own private railroad car, with both ends guarded by surly bastards with scatter guns. Makes it a bitch for the brakemen, having to climb over the damned car because they ain't allowed through it."

Longarm scowled down into his beer suds as he digested that. Smiley said, "They do say she ain't bad-looking, and she likely packs more in her purse than your average housewife. But, if you ask me, I'd say she was putting on airs. Trains don't get hit by Indians these days."

"No," Longarm said, "but they do have the Bacons out this way and the James-Younger gang farther east. I doubt the senator knows Jesse James all that well, and he does seem mighty fond of the pretty little thing. Does anyone know when she might grace Denver with her presence some more?"

Smiley said, "Yep. She's due back most any time. It ain't hard to track a private railroad car at a distance when you know a railroad dispatcher or two. Even a senator's wife has to give 'em some notice."

Dutch suggested, "We could set up a grand reception for her and them gunslicks, knowing when her train's due to arrive, you know."

Longarm shook his head and said, "Don't even consider it. They already have me on the carpet to answer for such rough justice. We don't have a thing on the bodyguards left. We can't throw down on nobody before they make the first hostile move."

Dutch looked sort of pouty as he protested, "That's a dumb way to deal with a gunslick, Longarm. I've always found it safer to shoot first and ask questions later."

"Not this time," Longarm insisted. "I've already got enough questions to answer about such past affairs. So I want you boys to steer clear of the whole bunch for now, and let me handle it as best I can figure."

They agreed reluctantly, so he finished his one beer and went home to his furnished digs. He went up to his hired corner room, shucked his sweaty duds, and made it to the next-door bath without having to explain why he was out in the hall in no more than a towel and six-gun. He locked himself in long enough for a short bath, a long crap, and a quick shave. Then he went back to his own room to get dressed some more, starting with clean underwear and a dab of Bay Rum under each armpit to deal with any stink he'd missed with that naptha soap.

Then, seeing he was off duty, and the night was

138

shaping up so balmy, he slipped into faded but clean jeans and a fresh hickory shirt. He had to put his tweed vest on again so he'd still have enough breast pockets for his smokes, timepiece, and derringer. Then he left as quietly as he'd come, sticking a match stem in the door crack under the bottom hinge before he locked up. He figured on sleeping alone, later, and while that could be painful enough, it could hurt worse to come home to an ambush.

As he legged it back across Cherry Creek and enjoyed a quick bite on the way, he studied some more on just who might be after him and why. For he couldn't get it to make solid sense.

His current fix had apparently started with that alley shoot-out with one of the senator's pet guns. So far so good, or at least a good motive for a bad man. But why would anyone want to tip their hand by summoning an enemy before a kangaroo court, if he was the head kangaroo, and then send paid assassins after him? Anyone with a lick of sense should be able to see that having a lawman gunned after you'd announced in the *Denver Post* that you meant to have his badge would put you at the top of the suspects list.

As he paid up and left in the gathering dust, Longarm told an alley fence he was resting against, "Dove came after me after the senator's wife fired him. He could have been rehired by somebody else. But Calhoun was for sure on their payroll, earlier. So I reckon we'd best walk alone and sharp until this odd situation *does* make sense."

His determination to leave sissy gals out of his fight didn't include his legal advisor, Amanda Bleeker, even if she was an old sissy gal. He'd told her he'd get back to her as soon as he knew anything. But, just the same, she seemed surprised to see Longarm when she came to her door, at last, in a fancier part of town than he could afford.

She said, "Oh, it's you. I wasn't expecting company at this hour, Custis."

He'd already surmised as much when she'd come to the door with her hair down, dressed in no more than a pale blue kimono. It was thanks to the lamplight shining through the thin silk from behind her that he could tell it was all she had on. He kept his eyes polite as he said, "I could come back another time if you have other company, ma'am."

She said, "Don't talk dirty. As a matter of fact, I was going over the charges against you just now, and, well, I can see by your shirtsleeves that you find it a warm evening as well."

There was a long awkward silence. Then she nodded and said, "Come in. We have a lot to talk about. I had no idea what I was getting into when Marshal Vail asked me to advise you."

As she led him back to a sort of den outfitted with a paper-cluttered writing table and overstuffed leather chesterfield, with law books glaring down at them from all sides, he asked if she had any good suggestions yet. She waved him to a seat on the chesterfield, perched her own thinly clad rump on a stool by the table, and said, "Yes. You might begin by turning in your badge and moving to Alaska. I see that in your time you've declared war on both Canada and Mexico."

He put his hat aside and grinned up at her sheepishly as he explained, "El Presidente Diaz don't hate me personal. He just hates all gringo lawmen."

She repressed a smile as she replied, "Just the same, you have to admit you overdid it down Mexico way the time you peppered a Mexican field artillery battalion with its own cannon."

He shrugged and said, "They was hauling them big guns to pepper folk I liked better. Does Senator Winger have *that* down against me? I felt sure I'd wiped out all them federales."

She sniffed and said, "Nobody can say you didn't try. And why on earth did you ever tangle with the Northwest Mounted Police that time?"

"Which time are they talking about?" he asked. "The MacDonald administration they got up Canada way right now seems to enjoy pouting at Uncle Sam for some reason."

She said, "I'd have to agree that with U.S. lawmen like you jumping back and forth across their border un-invited, Canada may have a reason to pout. They've accused you of aiding and abetting Louis Riel's rebel movement and kidnapping Canadian citizens! How are we going to answer that?"

He shrugged and said, "Not guilty. Both ways. As a U.S. lawman I had no call to arrest anyone up there trying to overthrow a stuffy government that admits it just don't like Uncle Sam. As for arresting a few old boys who ran home to hide behind the mounties after committing crimes in the U.S. of A., I felt that was only my duty. I get along with some mounties. Hey, I've even met a couple of decent Mex lawmen in my time. But most of the time, I've found it simpler to just track my wants down wherever they might be and bring 'em back dead or alive, their choice."

She wrinkled her nose and said, "Marshal Vail thinks he can square things with Kansas and Colorado about that informal exit with Big Bob Bacon from the State-line jail. Senator Winger is sure to bring it up, anyway. What about that time you pistol-whipped a Texas Ranger and stole his prisoner from him?"

He said, "Aw, that was just another dumb jurisdictional dispute. He was the one being dumb. The cuss we were both after was wanted federal and later, after Billy Vail talked to some old Ranger pals, they dropped the charges against me."

She waved a sheet of notepaper and said, "Not according to that congressional committee. I've already checked off a lot of wild accusations that we ought to be able to field, even though the crowd they'll be playing to is sure to take you for a homicidal lunatic with a mean streak. Whether justified or not, Custis, you have to admit you take the dead in dead-or-alive above and beyond the call of duty."

He shook his head and objected, "That simply ain't true, Amanda. My outfit makes a habit of sending me into rough country after rough customers. I really don't enjoy the company of a dead man after the first full day on the trail. But a man has to be sort of desperate to run off to such rough parts and, well, even when I *try* to just wing 'em, it's often just not possible to get them to a doc before they give up the ghost on me."

"I was wondering why they called you their long arm," she said. "I think I understand. But I know how bad I could make you look if *I* was chairing that committee, and that mean old senator seems to really have it in for you!"

He nodded and said, "I noticed. I've been studying on that."

He brought her up to date on all the legwork he'd done on the Wingers that afternoon. She even made a few notes. But when he'd finished she said, "You're right. It makes no sense. Even if your suspicion that Winger knew those train robbers were using his rock quarry as a hideout could be proven, the senator still went about it all wrong. Had not that bodyguard of his

142

picked a fight with you, before you had any reason to suspect anything—"

"I still wouldn't suspect anything," he cut in. "I don't see how they could have known I'd be sent to pick up Big Bob, or that I'd be able to get him to talk."

She shook her head and said, "They could have, knowing your reputation as Billy Vail's ace deputy. A respectable politician, tied in with mad-dog outlaws, running for reelection, might act mad-dog on mere suspicion, it's true. But the dates just don't work at all!"

He asked what dates she had in mind and she waved a sheaf of notes at him, saying, "Senator Winger announced his inquiry into your rough notions of justice weeks ago, naming you as his main target. That was *before* Big Bob Bacon tangle-footed himself into the arms of the law in Stateline, see?"

He said, "I do now. You're right. The cuss was out to kangaroo me, on my rep alone, before there was any chance I'd get to question Big Bob. But hold on. That untrustworthy member of the gang *did* get picked up just before Calhoun tried to gun me in that alley. What if, having started a feud with me, they wanted to end it, sudden?"

She shook her head, apparently unaware how open her kimono had fallen, and said, "Winger wouldn't have had to have you murdered to avoid ever meeting you. As the chairman of the committee he selected, he could have simply dropped the matter. Would you have dug into his past as much as you have if he'd just said it was all a mistake and gone back to Washington?"

"Not hardly," he said. "Billy Vail works me hard enough as it is. But I'd have still gone to Stateline and I'd have still had a crack at finding out the Bacons were hiding out on property the senator owns." She shook her head again, exposing even more of herself to view, as she insisted, "Ask yourself which would be more of a risk, Custis, ordering one of your hired guns to go up against a lawman of your rep, or ordering the same man to ride over to that quarry and warn the people there to clear out for a while? Even if Calhoun had killed you, there'd have been a thorough investigation that could have led back to the senator via his own employee. But what if they'd just decided to forget all about you and gone back to Washington, as you suggested?"

He thought, chuckled, and said, "Not a thing they had to worry about. I'd have never given the senator another thought. I'd have just gone to Stateline to pick up Big Bob, and even if he'd led us to that quarry, we'd have figured he was greening us to stall for time and forgot about that, too, once we'd found nobody there! You sure are smart. I could kiss you for thinking so hard and clear for me."

She lowered her lashes and leaned her elbows back on the table as she asked softly but sort of sassy, "Can't you do better than that, Custis?"

So after he'd sprung up to kiss her, one hand slipping inside her kimono with a mind of its own, she murmured, "Not in here, dear. I'm simply not built for tabletop loving, and that chesterfield just isn't big enough for both of us."

He laughed, scooped her up in his arms, and headed on out before asking where they might be going. She laughed too, told him there was no might about it and, sure enough, they wound up in a bedroom just down the hall. Her kimono was wide open by the time he lowered her to the counterpane. So he only had to get his gun rig off and his jeans down before they were mighty good friends. She didn't fret about his scratchy tweed vest until they'd gotten the first ferocious get-to-know-each-other out of the way, moaning and groaning with delight. Then she must have really wanted to get at him with her nails, because she insisted they both strip total and crawl under the covers to do it decent. It was she who kicked the covers off the bed atop his boots and duds before they climaxed together a second time. He was brought up too polite to ask to what he owed such unexpected pleasure. But, being female, she must have figured some explanations were in order. So as they lay there panting for their second winds, with both his cheroot and her bedroom lamp lit, she sighed and said, "You must think I'm just awful. But I couldn't let you go back out there in the dark with Lord knows who after you and the hearing starting tomorrow morning."

He snuggled her bare chest closer to his and said, "I'd have complained if I thought you did it awful and, while I'm not all that afraid of the dark, this sure has going home, getting up, and coming back all over again beat by miles. You were expecting this more than I was, right?"

She kissed his bare chest and sighed, "Your wild and wicked ways with women were something else I was going to have to go over with you, if you hadn't gotten just as wild and wicked as they say you are, sooner than I dared hope. What gave me away, answering the door half undressed?"

He said, "Well, I had told you I was coming. So even if you hadn't planned on my coming the way we just did, I found you ready for bed a mite early."

She sighed and said, "I can see a girl just has no secrets from you. What's the story about you and that murderess over on Lincoln Avenue? Did you get her to confess this way?"

He grimaced and replied, "Not guilty, your honor. I suspected her of trying to poison me before she managed to. That's why she drank the poison herself. I wish the *Post* hadn't written that case up so lurid. It's dumb for a lawman to make love to a suspect. That's why I didn't do it. I was out to arrest her platonic."

She said, "I'm glad. But according to the awesome dossier the senator's gathered on you, there have been times when you were charged by a woman you brought in alive of, well, taking advantage of your position."

He moved her into a better position and got rid of his smoke as he told her. "The best position for anyone I arrest, male or female, is handcuffed. I just said it was dumb to give 'em a chance to compromising an arresting officer. Whether we do or we don't, half the gals we bring in say we raped 'em or worse."

As he remounted to enter her again Amanda gasped in mingled pleasure and awe, then asked, "What would you call worse than rape, not letting them enjoy it?"

He began to move in and out of her teasingly as he said, "I just had to bust a man's neck for trying to prove this motion could be less pleasant. But I ain't figuring on ever having to arrest you, so let's not gossip about my past and I won't ask where you learned to do this so good, either."

She wrapped her slender but strong legs around his waist and hugged him tighter, her nails digging into his bare buttocks a mite harder than she needed to spur him into a full gallop. By the time he was there again she seemed to be leaping fences with him. As she climaxed, whipping her long black hair from side to side across the fresh linen, he returned the compliment and went limp in her loving arms until it occurred to him he could be too heavy for her and started to roll off. But she held him tightly and murmured, "No. Don't move. I'm not quite back down from heaven yet. Do you feel compromised, darling?"

He kissed her throat and muttered, "Not yet. But, at

this rate, I'll just never be able to arrest you, come morning."

She giggled and said, "I'm glad. I've a couple of other things I'd like to try with you that just happen to be against statute law in this state. Are you really as wild and wicked as they say you are, Custis?"

He chuckled and said, "I don't know how any man of mortal clay could be. But if you're out to establish a legend, I'm game."

Chapter 10

She was. It seemed sort of a shame their legendary night would never be recorded in print, lest it start a fire. But for a gal who could act so wild in bed, old Amanda looked cool as a cucumber, if not downright severe, by the time she'd fed him breakfast in bed and they'd done it one last time in her bathtub before getting dressed. She naturally put on her black courtroom outfit and proved she was like lots of other women, after all, by chiding him about his own appearance.

She said, "Honestly, dear, you can't really mean to appear before the committee on the opera house stage wearing jeans and a work shirt!"

"If it was up to me," he said, "I wouldn't appear in a stovepipe hat and a claw-hammer coat. No matter how I show up, they mean to make me look like a wild man from Borneo, right?"

She sighed and said, "That's all too true. But you don't have to meet them halfway. I wish we had time to get you back into that suit you really ought to be wearing with that vest. You look like you just drove a herd into town."

He said, "I had a hard night. My sissy duds are clean over on the far side of the creek, and if they mean to crucify me I may as well dress comfortable. Do you want to walk or shall I go out and rustle us up a hack?"

"The opera house is only a few blocks away," she said, "and I want to talk to you a lot before we get there. Last night, every time I tried to rehearse you on your testimony, I seemed to wind up coming again."

He chuckled fondly and said, "That was a lot more fun than rehearsing testimony. I've appeared in court a lot of times, so don't worry. I know better than to spit on the floor or even in the judge's eye."

As they headed down the hall toward her front door she took his arm and warned, "Try to keep it in mind that these hearings won't be a regular court proceeding. We'll be seated together at a table, facing the panel. They won't be quite within your spitting range, I hope. Try to say as little as possible and when in doubt, ask me before you answer."

He said, "I only mean to tell the truth."

"Don't you dare. Your best bet is to plead the fifth and let them lash at you until they run out of breath. Nothing you say will be recorded in your favor and anything you say may be used against you, see?"

"No," he said. "Won't I look like a liar if I hide behind the constitution like a man with something to hide?"

She reached ahead to unlock the front door with her key as she explained, "They're going to call you a liar and worse no matter what you say."

Outside, the morning air was fresh and some fresh

birds were tweeting cheerfully. But it didn't cheer Longarm as Amanda went on in much the same vein as she walked him the short distance to his impending ordeal.

According to her, when a bunch of congressmen got together to tongue-lash folks suspected of most anything, they were no more bound by a suspect's constitutional rights or even common courtesy than the lions Nero had fed those Christians to had been.

She explained, "When a regular trial judge really rides roughshod over a client's constitutional rights, a smart lawyer can appeal to a higher court. But Winger and his lickspittles have congressional immunity. Even if we could prove them guilty of outright criminal libel they'd have the excuse that, since the hearings are not an actual trial, they were only speaking informal."

He asked, "Don't that give me the right to sass 'em back?"

"Don't you dare! *You* don't have congressional immunity. So they can cite you for contempt of congress if you don't mind your manners."

He growled, "That just ain't fair."

She answered with a curt nod of agreement. "Windy Winger isn't out to fight anyone fair. He's out to make himself look good at your expense. Try to remember he's playing to the audience and newspaper reporters, not you or me, and try to give him as little to twist as you can without actually refusing to answer. Our only hope of revenge lies in keeping those newspaper columns as short as we can by giving them less to print. Maybe, once he sees he's not going to get enough front-page space by tormenting you, he'll go on to call somebody else before his panel."

Longarm frowned and asked, "Like who?"

When she told him, "You can't be the only western lawman who ever pistol-whipped anyone, dear," he made up his mind to go down with the ship. For nobody but a rat would subject good old boys like Smiley and Dutch to cruel and unusual punishment at the hands of a mess of jabbering dudes.

They swung the last corner to spy a considerable crowd gathered in front of the opera house. They circled wide to duck down the side alley leading to the stage entrance. But when they got there they found another albeit smaller crowd milling about in a haze of impatient cigar smoke.

Billy Vail was there, along with Crawford of the *Post* and some other reporters, and a sketch artist with a big pad of art paper and a fistful of charcoal crayons. He commenced to sketch Longarm's arrival as Vail scowled at him and demanded, "Is that any way to dress for a select committee, dammit?"

Longarm said, "I never selected 'em and I can sweat better in these jeans. How come we're all standing out here like this? Ain't it close to nine?"

Crawford, a heavyset gent in a sport striped jacket and a straw summer hat, took the stogie out of his cherubic face to say, "It's after nine and we're still waiting for the grand entrance. I wish *I* had a job I couldn't get fired from, taking my own damned time."

Another, older newspaperman said, "Old Windy was even late for his last wedding. But at least we all got to sit inside the church while we waited for the slugabed."

Billy Vail and Longarm exchanged glances. They were both nosy lawmen by nature. Longarm asked, "How come you said *last* wedding? Senator Winger ain't a Mormon, is he?"

The reporter shrugged and said, "If he is, he picked the wrong church to marry up with Miss Regina eight or nine years ago. It wasn't bigamy, more's the pity. I understand he was married years ago, before the war, to

152

some gal who died in childbirth, child and all. Like I said, he married Miss Regina long after he came west. Some say he had to. Sorry, ma'am, but facts is facts. He *was* late to their wedding, and drunk when he showed up."

Crawford seemed aware of Amanda as well when he nudged his rival and said, "Don't pass gossip on unless you know it to be news. The Wingers never had no kids, early or late, after they married up. A man has a right to get a little drunk when he's fixing to marry up with a woman like Regina Winger."

Longarm asked, "Do you know the lady, Crawford?"

The man he knew as a reliable reporter replied, "Not as well as her poor husband does, praise the Lord. She ain't bad-looking for a gal her age, but she bosses him around as if he was her poodle dog. Maybe he *is* her poodle dog. He don't seem to *mind* her bossy ways. The hired help at the Palace can't stand her. One chambermaid confided in me that old Regina can yell like a banshee once she's liquored up, but that the senator just takes it as if he had cotton stuffed in his ears."

Closer to Longarm, in a softer tone, Amanda Bleeker told Longarm, "We could be in luck. Everyone knows his wife is the driving force behind Senator Winger. With her out of town, he could be having second thoughts about these hearings. It's no secret that you're popular here in Denver. By this time he must know it."

Crawford proved he had sharp ears by saying, "If he's changed his mind, she'll change it *back* for him soon enough. Her nibs is due back from Washington this morning. Her private car should have rolled into the yards by now."

Billy Vail hauled out his watch to cuss at it and mutter, "I just hate a henpecked bully. My old woman knows better than to get *me* off to the office late. How long does the fool expect us to wait?"

Before Longarm could reply that he meant to get it over with today one way or the other, Sergeant Nolan, Denver P.D., entered the alley astride a big police bay, leading a spare mount. He called out, "Longarm, you're wanted over to the railroad yards. Senator Winger asked for you by name."

Longarm asked, "Do tell? I thought they wanted to crucify me *here,* this morning."

Nolan said, "That was before. Less than an hour ago the fancy private railroad car that was carrying Regina Winger back from Washington rolled in. She wasn't aboard it. All four of her private bodyguards were, riddled with bullets. So right now the senator is beside himself with worry about his wife and he knows you're the best lawman in these parts. So he wants you to track down his old woman and her abductors, right now if not sooner."

Vail grinned like a mean little kid and said, "Hell, let's make him beg." But Longarm was already mounting up. He knew the trail was already cold enough as it was. No matter how he felt about a political windbag and his pushy wife, they were still human beings in a lot of trouble.

Longarm and Nolan had to step over a body just inside the forward entrance of the varnished maroon private car to get to where Senator Winger was seated in a sort of dinky drawing room with his head in his hands. As he looked up hopefully, Longarm saw he looked older or a lot more worried than his official photgraphs. The senator sobbed, "They took her, Lord knows where, or what they're *doing* to her right now! You've got to *find* her, Deputy Long!"

154

Longarm said, "I can only try. We're talking about a couple of thousand miles of tracks between here and Washington. So for openers, are you sure your wife ever got on?"

Winger asked what sort of a question that was and Longarm said, "A smart one. Have you tried wiring home to make sure she ain't having tea in the garden right now?"

The old man looked bewildered as Nolan told Longarm, *"We've* already wired D.C.P.D. That was basic. Even better, we know she was aboard as far west as Kansas City. A brakeman wanted to pass through the car and got yelled at a lot. The deed had to be done somewhere on the prairie in the wee small hours, last night. The train crew noticed nobody was on guard as usual when they stopped to jerk water at Limin, say, seventy-five miles east. They thought nothing of it, seeing it was none of their business, until they got here around six, rolled this private car off on a siding, and forgot about it. The senator here found the bodies when he came over around eight-thirty to see what was keeping the lady and her party."

"It was awful," the senator moaned. "At first I thought they might have murdered my Regina, too. But her sleeping compartment was empty, thank God and curse whoever took her!"

Longarm said, "All right, stay put, both of you, whilst I have a prowl about these narrow premises."

Leaving Nolan to comfort the missing woman's husband, Longarm did just that. The frilly as well as largest sleeping compartment contained the slept-in but empty bunk bed he'd been led to expect. An empty compartment right next to it held a made-up bunk and smelled stuffy, as if nobody had used it recently. That had to be a guest accommodation, or where the senator got to

155

sleep when he was traveling with his wife and she was complaining of a headache. He knew lots of old married couples slept separate, even when they were still going at it two or three times a week. For once the first thrill of sleeping with a snorer wore off, one tended to be practical about getting a good night's sleep. There was a luggage compartment filled with expensive luggage. The woman had left the train with no more than she might have had on at the time. If she'd changed duds on her way out and off, there'd have been a nightgown or whatever hung or flung more casual in her compartment.

Closer to the front end of the car Longarm slid open a door just a few yards back from the body he'd already seen and could still see sprawled in the companionway. Inside he found two bunk beds. Servants didn't get to sleep as grand as the folk they worked for. The two guards who'd been sleeping, or at least undressed for bed when they'd died, were still there. One lay on the top bunk with a little blue hole in his temple and his brains spattered all over the far paneling. The other lay facedown on the deck near his bottom bunk. Longarm didn't have to roll him over to determine he'd been hit four times at close range. The rounds had gone out his back. From the still-sticky blood spattered on one bulkhead, Longarm could tell he'd made it to his feet before the killer opened up on him. He muttered, "Yep, you boys were off duty when one or more rascals simply stepped in shooting. That means they got your pards on guard first. But no more than a few seconds first, or you'd have both been wide awake, right?"

Neither answered. He went back outside to move all the way aft, ignoring the shaken senator and Nolan, to find the fourth bodyguard. The compartment at that end was fixed up as a sort of rolling dining room, with food

156

and no doubt drinks served across a bar between there and the tiny kitchen tucked just forward. Longarm saw the dead man had been hit thrice. But he'd died harder than the others, trying to crawl back from the door on his shot-up belly. One outstretched hand was bloody, the source of the blood no mystery. But the smears he'd made on the mock-oriental rug with a bloody fingertip seemed worth a hunker down. So Longarm hunkered, and by squinting just so at the barely visible letters drawn in blood on the maroon, black, and lighter blue pile, he figured them for a *D* followed by an *O*. A brand? Or the start of a longer message the poor cuss simply hadn't been able to manage?

Longarm rejoined Nolan and the senator. Noticing a liquor cabinet in one corner, he hunkered down to open it. As he was regarding the stock of bottles, opened and unopened, the senator snarled, "For God's sake, are you going to search for Regina or get drunk?"

"Don't get your bowels in an uproar, old son," Longarm said. "I like to eat the apple a bit at a time. Were your hired help allowed at this private stock?"

Old Winger growled, "Not if they knew what was good for them and, now that you mention it, I suppose we *could* all use a nip about now."

Longarm said, "I reckon it's safe to nip from a sealed bottle. Nolan, I want the contents of all these bottles assayed by your police lab. What are we drinking this morning, Senator?"

Winger said he took his bourbon neat if he couldn't get any branch water. So Longarm hauled out a sealed fifth of the same and shut the cabinet. As he straightened up, tearing off the seal and opening the bottle with his teeth, he searched for any sign of glasses but found none. He handed the bottle to their upset host, saying, "There you go. There's something I don't understand

157

about the way you and your lady used to travel. How come there were four bodyguards but not one cook or chambermaid to pick up after everyone?"

Senator Winger sucked on the bottle like a big baby before he lowered it with a wheeze to explain, "We were too short on space. This car was only built to accommodate a serving staff of half a dozen and, as you can see, bodyguards were more important to us. The longest trip we could manage, coast to coast, seldom took more than a workday week, and Regina found it a change to do the cooking and such while we were on the road."

Nolan looked smug as he said, "Had there been any servants slaughtered along with them guards, I feel sure we'd have noticed them by now, Longarm."

The taller and more naturally suspicious lawman in the room said, "You cover all bets before you flap your mouth, Sarge. I like to get a grip on where a trail might start before I try to follow it. I know it sounds like a dumb question, but is it safe to assume nobody even tried to stop this train last night as it rolled cross-country in the dark, doing forty to sixty miles an hour?"

Nolan said, "You're right. That's a dumb question." But then he brightened and said, "Hey, that's right. There was just no way the kidnappers could have boarded a speeding train. Don't that narrow her down to the few places it had to stop at least long enough to jerk boiler water?"

Longarm nodded and said, "The railroad will know better where and when they even slowed down. You can save me some legwork by picking up a timetable and wiring every place they might have heard some gunfire last night. Small-town folk tend to turn over and go back to sleep after hearing distant gunshots. But they can often recall them, if they're asked, later."

Nolan said, "Consider it done. Our coroner would sure like to get at them bodies, any time you have no further use of 'em."

Longarm shrugged and said, "I wasn't fixing to bury anybody." But then he asked the senator, "Do the letters *D* and *O* mean anything to you? One of Miss Regina's bodyguards wrote them in his own blood. Could be a cattle brand, or the start of some name."

Winger took another swig of the bourbon and hugged the bottle to him as if it was all his to keep and cherish, which it was, when you studied on it. He said, "My herds are all branded Flying W. I don't recall a D.O. brand."

Nolan offered to check that out with the state brand inspector. Longarm said, "You'd best contact the Cattleman's Protective Association. We could be talking about an out-of-state brand if the dying man spotted it on a pony."

Nolan grimaced and said, "All right. But I can't say I like the C.P.A. They got too many hired guns on their payroll to suit my taste."

"All the more reason to compare notes with them," Longarm said. "If someone's missing a cow pony wearing such a brand, *they'd* be looking for it too, just as serious."

He turned back to Winger and tried, "What about the start of a name, Senator? Have you ever had anything to do with someone who's name or even nickname might commence with them letters?"

Winger shook his head and said, "I've already thought about that. I just can't see Senator Douglas kidnapping my Regina at gunpoint, can you?"

Longarm smiled thinly and said, "I reckon we're talking about someone more athletic. Let's not chaw that bite no more for now. As I read the signs of female dressing, your woman was up and dressed when she got off the train, wherever. Is she an early riser, as a rule?"

Winger shrugged and said, "It depends. You know how women are. I've seen her sleep past noon after entertaining guests. On the other hand, she's been known to rise before cock's crow to get at the bugs in the garden out back. Does it really *matter* what time she got up this morning?"

Longarm looked disgusted and said, "The train crew would have surely noticed a passenger getting off in broad daylight on wide-open prairie. She was up and dressed before dawn, unlss we consider her getting off here in Denver, *after* this car was uncoupled and run up this otherwise deserted siding."

They both stared at him thunderghasted. Nolan said, "Longarm, that's a wild notion, even coming from you. Are you saying the kidnapping took place right here on my very own beat in broad-ass daylight?"

Longarm shook his head and said, "We won't know for sure until we cover all the other stops this side of Kansas City. But the train stopped here as well. Have you canvassed the neighborhood for sounds of early-morning gunfire, here beyond the stockyards, where folks are used to drunken cowhands?"

Nolan said, "I have not. But I surely shall. Wouldn't a gang have to be bold as hell to smoke up a parked car and frog march a famous lady off across the tracks at gunpoint?"

Longarm nodded and said, "I can't see a bunch of *sissies* gunning four hired guns in *any* neck of the woods."

Senator Winger stared up at them in mingled hope and fear to ask, "Are you suggesting my poor Regina could be being held somewhere in this very city?"

Longarm said, "I don't know where the lady is. When someone can be most anywhere, I like to start by searching closest to where they could be."

He reached for a cheroot, since it was obvious nobody was going to offer him a drink around here, and said, "I want you to go back to your hotel and sit tight, Senator. If anyone has any sensible reasons for abducting your woman, they'll likely send you a ransom note. If they ain't after money they must be after something else. No offense, but men hardly ever kidnap middle-aged women so noisy just to admire 'em."

He turned back to Nolan and said, "I'll check back with you later at headquarters. Between your crew and mine, we ought to be able to at least eliminate her being here in Denver."

Nolan said, "Denver's a big town."

"I know. That's why I'd best get moving. You boys question your usual informants and my boys will question some you might not know about. Headquarters, quitting time?"

Nolan nodded and Longarm turned to go. But Senator Winger felt obliged to blurt out, "Longarm, about that little misunderstanding we might have had about your, ah, methods..."

Longarm turned to scowl down at him as he replied, "There was no misunderstanding. You was out to make yourself look bigger by tearing me down. Lots of folk who ain't even out to make newspaper headlines disapprove of rough justice until *they're* in the market for some. It's sure surprising how a sweet little old lady can chide the law for arresting her drunken grandson on one occasion and holler for blood the moment someone she don't know walks across her flower bed. But such bullshit goes with the badge I tote. If your woman's still alive we'll find her. If she ain't, we'll be proud to hang the sons of bitches for you. I just don't want to hear no more of your bullshit about needless brutality when this is over, hear?"

Senator Winger assured him soberly that he could gut-shoot or even scalp the sons of bitches who'd taken his dear Regina, as long as Longarm got her back. So Longarm lit his smoke, adjusted the .44-40 on his hip for easier walking, and left to track the fool woman down.

After that it got more complicated. By noon Longarm sensed he was moving in circles. For though he was following the usual routine, he'd visited the same places and sent the same wires as he had the day before when he'd been trying to get something *on* Senator Winger. He hadn't worked as hard on the now-missing wife. There wasn't near as much to find out about her. That was perhaps why he was having such a tough time picturing her. Sure, he knew what she looked like, thanks to those morgue photographs, and while he'd established she might not be the sort of old gal he'd like to play slap-and-tickle with, there was nothing tying her into the Bacon clan. It hardly seemed likely they'd want to kidnap one of their own if she *was* tied in with them.

He found himself legging it up Colfax Avenue before he got around to considering why. All the state-house records up on the crest of the hill had been gone over to no avail. You had to *catch* kidnappers before you could ask to see any *records* they might have. He'd already gone through the county records on poor old Regina the day before, down at the civic center. His pal, the widow woman on Sherman Avenue, lived on the far side of the capitol grounds and he wasn't feeling horny anyway, so that was no reason to be trudging up such a slope at high noon.

Then he got to the corner of Colfax and Sherman, nodded to himself, and swung north, not south, along the tree-shaded and wind-swept avenue, lined by imposing brownstones. He came to one with the horse-headed hitching post out front painted pink and turned in. He mounted the imposing steps and twisted the door bell. A few minutes later a flustered looking lady of middle age and heroic proportions came to the door in her own kimono with her own dark hair down. Her resemblance to Amanda Bleeker ended right there, and he knew she hadn't been expecting him. She hadn't even been expecting one of her music pupils unless they'd graduated to the French horn. But, of course, that was more than possible, allowing for her lusty nature.

Mavis Weatherwax was a horny old gal his fairly regular lover, down the avenue a piece, had warned him not to play with. The big brunette was a widow woman, too. Or maybe, as some said, it was true a mining mogul had agreed to a handsome divorce settlement in exchange for her promise to leave him the hell alone.

But old Mavis wasn't hard to take in small doses. A weekend with her would likely hospitalize the average man. But she sure offered swell quickies.

As she hauled him inside and kissed him, Mavis gasped, "What are you doing here in blue jeans? What will the neighbors think?"

He hugged her back and told her, "Nothing, if we don't let 'em watch. But to tell the truth I came more for conversation than one of your swell piano lessons, honey. Is there some place we can talk?"

She led him into her parlor, tossed her kimono atop the grand piano tucked into a bay window, and laid down on the rug, stark naked, to say, "Sure. What do you want to talk about, Custis?"

He sat down on the piano bench. It was easier to do

163

that after the night he'd spent with another sex-crazed brunette. He said, "I hope you won't take this as an insult, Mavis, but one time in a moment of passion you let slip your approximate age, and allowed you'd come west as a kid when this town was still the mining camp of Cherry Creek."

She put her hefty thighs back together as she pouted up at him, "What of it? You told me that time you admired women of some experience, you brute."

He said, "Oh, I do. I was just wondering if you might have known another gal called Regina Masterson, growing up at about the same time in what was still a mighty small town."

The now somewhat older small-town girl on the rug said, "I may recall the name. We're talking a long time back when I was less anxious to screw. What are you waiting for? I've told you before that my nosy neighbors count the minutes between a critter in pants walking in and out my front door."

He began to shuck as he sighed and said, "Well, I don't want to ruin your rep with the neighbors." He was too polite to add her neighbors had to be deaf if they hadn't heard talk that had gotten all the way to that other widow woman who enjoyed his company, a backyard fence at a time, for a good half mile.

Once dressed the same way as old Mavis, Longarm lowered himself aboard her and then all a man had to do was hang on and pray as she love-bucked on the rug. They were making the whole house shake by the time she'd climaxed under him. Thanks to such earlier hard riding with a younger and prettier gal the night before, Longarm was just getting inspired by the time she went limp and just sort of laid there like a sort of *bare* skin rug, pun intended.

As she opened her eyes with a dreamy smile, to find

him still aroused by her big old bulges, Mavis marveled, "Oh, again? You really must have wanted me today, or is this just your way of getting me to gossip about poor little Regina the Rag Doll?"

He said, "Both, if you remember her now. How come you called her a rag doll? Wasn't she pretty as a kid?"

Mavis said, "Pretty as a mud pie, with no shape at all. Let me up, dammit. We have to keep the neighbors guessing. You know the meaning of my madness from last time, right?"

He did. It made him laugh as he withdrew and helped her to her feet. She moved swiftly over to the piano bench to kneel on it, her big rump thrust out to him so he could grasp an ample hip in each hand and enter her again, from behind, while she braced herself with one hand against the music rack and began to run the scales on the keyboard with her other. As he started moving it in her, in time with her playing, she began to play faster, but since one good turn deserved another, she asked him what on earth he might want with Regina the Rag Doll, since what they were doing seemed out of the question.

"She must have blossomed some as she finished with her awkward age," he said. "But I ain't out to do *this* to her. I'm trying to find her for her husband. She's been lost, strayed, or stolen and . . . hold the thought, I'm coming!"

She said she was too, and hit a loud crescendo as if to prove it. Then she sobbed, "Don't take it out. Can't we talk just as well like this as on my sofa?"

He doubted that, but it was her house. So he stayed in the same now-awkward position as she picked absently on the keys while he explained the situation about Regina Winger nee Masterson.

Once he'd convinced her he was searching for the missing woman with a pure heart, Mavis said, "Well, I never. I'd heard Windy Winger married up with some Leadville gal named Regina. I just never connected the two names. You see, all our crowd was wedded, or at least having fun, by the time that poor spinster gal moved up to Leadville. I think her father left her a mine, a chicken farm or whatever. It surely couldn't have been a house of ill repute. She was scared of boys and vice versa. A man would have to be mighty hard up to settle for old Rag Doll when sheep are so plentiful out this way."

Longarm began to move in her experimentally as he mused, "Oh, I don't know. Some gals blossom later than others. How old would she have been when she became a young gal of independent means?"

Mavis said, "Faster, dammit. I'll bet *she* never got it like this. I guess she must have been somewhere in her late twenties last time I passed her on the street. That would have been over ten years ago. So I don't see how she could have gotten any better looking since. If a gal ain't good-looking by the time she's pushing thirty, there's just no hope for her."

Longarm frowned down at her naked spine as he mused aloud, "Her husband ain't the only one as finds her sort of good-looking as well as well preserved. You sure you and the other young gals weren't, well, jealous of her?"

Mavis arched her spine to take him deeper as she purred, "Oh, bless you for calling me a young gal. There was nothing for me and my friends to feel jealous about. She wasn't even rich, then. If we felt anything for such a lump it was pity. It wasn't that we didn't *like* poor little Regina. She was puppy-dog friendly and ever ready to help out if there was a Sunday Meeting-on-the-

Green or we were gathering poor-baskets for the trash kids across the creek. She was just one of them poor shy souls who seem doomed to die virgins and— You say she married up, after all? Well, I'm glad for her. She was a sweet little nothing who deserved something out of life and— Ooooh, I think I'm getting my *own* just desserts again, you sweet-donging man!"

He brought her to climax. He didn't know what *he* was doing in there anymore. But since she didn't ask him to take it out he left it where it was and muttered, "I'm missing something here. I know the camera can lie. I know a happy marriage can do wonders for some women. But the Regina Winger I know on sight, sort of, just don't look like a desperate spinster to me."

Mavis asked him where he'd ever seen old Regina the Rag Doll. So he told her, "They got her photograph on file at the *Post*. A close-up and another of her and the senator getting hitched."

Mavis began to gyrate her big hips for him as she said in a surprisingly conversational tone, "I didn't know they could print regular photographs in the news-papers yet."

"They can't," he said. "They've got it almost worked out back east, but so far the results are mighty murky. Most of the pictures you see in the *Post* are woodcuts, made from photos by staff artists, see?"

She said, "No. Why would they want to take pictures of anyone if they can't *print* 'em?"

He explained, "Nobody at the *Post* took any pictures of the senator and his wife. Society swells just volunteer photoprints, in case the paper ever figures out how to run 'em and . . . son of a bitch, that could be worth a trip to Leadville, and it's sure been nice talking to you, Mavis!"

She sobbed, "You can't leave me in this position, you cruel-hearted beast!"

But he told her she looked just swell in that position as he dressed as quickly as he could, and, while she *threatened* to chase him down the avenue and throw him down in the first bushes they came to, she was only funning. She didn't even follow him to the door in that dition.

Chapter 11

The mountain mining-town of Leadville, seat of Lake
County, lay about eighty miles southeast of Denver as
the crow might fly. Trains flying slower and more seldom, it was yet another afternoon by the time Longarm
left Leadville and got off once again at Stateline. Had
there been a shady side of the Ogallala Trail cum Main
Street at that hour he'd have hugged it. Since there
wasn't, he just strode up the middle, keeping a wary eye
on the windows and rooftops on either side until he got
to the town lockup.

He found young Jimmy and his boss, Zeke Jennings,
inside. Considering Longarm's last visit to the premises,
they were good sports about it. Jimmy said nailing
down a new floor in the back had mucking a stable
licked. Zeke said the money order Longarm had wired
to them for new lumber had been neighborly, but added
that nobody cared to dig up Big Bob Bacon.

They both wanted to know what had brought him
back to Stateline. Longarm said, "Billy Vail wants me
to bring home the last of the Bacon clan. We're pretty

169

sure we've wiped out most of them, what with that un-planned and hence disastrous train robbery and a rock quarry we blew up. But at least one of 'em sent a tele-gram to Golden, Colorado, from right here in Stateline. It was a ruse. Knowing I'd surely check with Western Union, the sneak who pointed me out for the late Cyrus Dove wired nobody at all in Golden to lay a false trail. I did better when I pawed through county records in Leadville. Opposite direction. You boys got the all-points on Senator Winger's missing wife, I hope?"

Zeke nodded and said, "We did. We can't help you on that. Her train did stop here, maybe three minutes, around quarter to four in the morning. Most everyone in town was asleep. But our post office hands met the mail car with their buckboard. They feel sure they'd have noticed if someone else was shooting up a lady's body-guards to carry her, screaming or otherwise, from her private car to nowhere much."

Jimmy nodded and said, "There's a shortage of deep dark dungeons in Stateline, Longarm. This here is about the only place in town to hold a prisoner, and you proved last time even *we* have our limitations."

Zeke said, "Nobody rode in or out of town on horse-back at that hour. The town wasn't *that* asleep."

Longarm smiled thinly and said, "I figure those four guards must have been gunned before the train got here. While the train was chugging and rumbling enough to muffle the noise of shots being fired inside closed doors and windows. In the predawn dark any number of folk could have snuck off the rear end of the train without being spotted by the boys up around the mail car. They'd have had no reason to be gazing that way. The railroad tells us no passengers had expressed a desire to get off or on that train at such an ungodly hour."

Zeke shrugged and said, "All right. Say they boarded

that train sneaky while it was jerking water farther east. Say they attacked the gal's private car whilst the train was rolling fast and noisy. Say they just held the lady captive until the train stopped here, and then carried her off the rear platform, sort of discreet. Where in thunder could they have carried her after that?"

"That's what I mean to find out for sure," Longarm said. "You boys had best stay here. It's a federal case. It could turn out ugly, too."

The two part-timers exchanged wary glances. But young Jimmy felt honor-bound to ask, "Don't you think you could use some backup?"

Longarm patted his holster and said, "I got all the backup I need. You boys stay put. I mean it." Then he ducked back out into the dazzling sunlight and headed across the way.

As they watched him through the grimy window, Jimmy said, "He seems to be headed for the Rainbow Saloon. I wonder how come."

Zeke said, "He likely feels the need of a drink before he goes after them kidnappers. I know *I* would."

But when Longarm parted the batwings and strode up to the bar he shook his head at old Kevin and said, "It's a mite early in the day for me. Is Miss Etta about?"

She was. She came out from the back so sudden he felt it was safe to assume she'd spotted him some time back from her upstairs window. Longarm turned to hook both elbows over the bar, facing her and the modest crowd in the place as Etta joined him, murmuring, "It's about time you came back to me, you brute. I didn't know what could have happened to you when I awoke to find you gone."

Longarm smiled fondly down at her and said, "You drank more gin than I did that evening. It was Bombay gin, sort of rare as well as expensive. I found a half-

171

empty bottle of it in a liquor cabinet the other morning. But what I'm really puzzled about is the way you get your hair that color, so quick, both ways. Do you soak it in tea or something stronger?"

She blinked in surprise and asked, "What are you talking about? I'll have you know I'm a natural blonde, all over, as well you should know."

He nodded and said, "That's true. You're even blonder between your sweet thighs, which is contrary to nature when you study on it. To be blonde down yonder, a gal would have to have even lighter hair on her *head*. But let's not talk dirty no more. We can't charge you with tinting your hair. Even if we could, that's the least of the sneaky tricks you've been playing on us poor men."

He nodded at the man lounging against the bar on the far side of her and said, "Miss Etta, I'd like you to meet Deputy Guilfoyle. I asked him to come along because I feel you compromised me as the arresting officer, for which I sincerely thank you."

As she gasped and started to twist away, Guilfoyle grabbed her right wrist with one hand, snapped one steel loop of his handcuffs around it, and told her, "Miss Etta Bacon, I arrest you in the name of the law for the murder of Regina Masterson and Lord knows how many others."

Then all hell busted loose.

Old Kevin, behind the bar, must have thought Longarm and his sidekick, Guilfoyle, were mighty dumb to be paying him no mind as he hauled two big Walker conversion .45s into view above the polished mahogany. But old Smiley, seated in one corner across the way, had been watching him all the time. So Smiley fired first. His ball blew Kevin's right lung all over the mirror behind the bar and didn't do the mirror any good, either. As Kevin went down he got off one shot, which exploded out through the bar he'd fallen behind in a geyser of gunsmoke and mahogany shavings. Then another young gent, dressed cow, fired at Longarm from another corner before Dutch, at the far end of the bar, could blow the side of his head off.

As things got suddenly quiet, Longarm rolled back up into a sitting position from where he'd been prone in the sawdust to ask Guilfoyle if he was all right. Guilfoyle, flat on the floor with the handcuffed Etta sort of sprawled facedown between them, said, "I made it. I think this gal might not have."

Longarm crawled closer to roll the female prisoner on her back. That one round Kevin had put through the bar on the way down hadn't messed her back up too bad, going in just above her tailbone. But it sure had torn hell out of her lower abdomen as it passed out the front of her. Her eyelids were fluttering. Longarm said, 'Uncuff her. If she comes to, she's going to want both hands to grip her guts with."

Smiley clumped over to them, reloading, to say, "I'm sorry, Longarm. I wasn't expecting him to produce two guns, already cocked."

Longarm shrugged and said, "You done the best you knew how," as, down at the far end, the bead curtains parted and Deputy Flynn came to join them, looking confused and sort of disappointed as he took in the scene of carnage. By this time all the old boys who'd just stopped by for an early beer were long gone.

Flynn said, "It was like you figured, Longarm. I found that derby hat and a man's suit about the right size hid away in a carpetbag under her bed. All the other duds she had upstairs was female. Some sort of fancy."

Longarm didn't answer. The girl's eyes were open now. He was hoping her last words would clear a few details up. But she just screamed and screamed, until she died about an hour later.

Chapter 12

It was closer to sunset when Marshal Billy Vail caught Longarm and Amanda Bleeker holding hands across the table of the conference room down the hall from his office. As he joined them he said, "I see I got back here just in time. Senator Winger's identified the body you and the boys brung back from Stateline as that of his wife of many a year. They have him under sedation right now."

Longarm shrugged and said, "I told you it was her. It had to be, to make any sense at all."

Vail struck a match to relight his pungent stogie. The only thing to be said about his choice of brands is that they tended to go out a lot. When he had it reeking again, Vail said, "If you say and her husband says that lady in the Denver Morgue is Regina Winger, I'm in no position to argue. But how come she don't look like the lady in them official wedding portraits the Wingers gave the society editors?"

Longarm said, "It was Mrs. Winger who no doubt reluctantly sent those old prints when the *Post* kept begging for 'em. She handled all or most of the senator's correspondence. Left to himself, he was a self-made mining mogul who could hardly read or write. I should be stood in a corner under a dunce cap for not wondering why a somewhat younger Winger has on a prewar wedding outfit. But since all of the gals were short and blonde, and I hadn't been introduced to even *one* of 'em by the senator, I made the same mistake the *Post* did. When you ask a lady you don't really know for her picture, and she sends you a picture—"

"Hold on," Vail cut in, "you got the senator and me confused enough by bringing back his kidnapped wife as another dead gal entire. How in blue blazes does a *third* mysterious woman come into the picture?"

Longarm said, "Oh, the bride in those official wedding portraits ain't mysterious, Billy. She died shortly after she and Windy Winger married up, years ago. His *second* wife, the one we caught up with in Stateline, avoided having wedding pictures taken when she and Winger got hitched here in Denver, later. That was easy enough to determine. Had any Denver photographer taken such pictures they'd have had a *record* of it, see?"

Vail looked blank. Amanda brightened and said, "I think I do. That two-faced thing wouldn't have dared pose for pictures if she was a member of an outlaw clan. But later, after she'd gotten used to being a rich society lady, and the society editors kept badgering her for background material, she assumed that since one old photo of a vapid blonde looked much the same as any other, once it was reproduced as a woodcut—"

"Now *you're* doing it!" Vail cut in. "Never mind why a gal with no pictures of her ownself handy might settle for a couple of another gal entire. Regina Masterson was no member of no outlaw nothing. She was brung up

176

by kind parents, right here in Denver. She made it to mature spinsterhood without even busting a window, and they say she went to church regular, too."

Longarm nodded and said, "Everyone who can recall the poor plain gal at all agrees she was virtuous to a fault. She never had no boyfriends and she was too shy to have any real girlfriends. She was just a pleasant blur who helped out at church socials and such until her dull mother passed away and her dull father made a modest strike up near Leadville. When he died in turn, she moved up to Lake County to manage or dispose of the estate. Nobody here in Denver noticed."

"Oh, the poor girl," Amanda murmured.

Longarm nodded and said, "It gets worse. For while the plain Regina was growing up shy and no doubt lonesome in the city, a somewhat younger and much prettier Etta Bacon was growing up wild in the mountains. *She* got along *fine* with boys. She was a slice above most of the Bacons when it came to brains. But she'd been raised to be as sly and sneaky. Somehow, Regina Masterson and Etta Bacon got to be pals up in Leadville. It wouldn't have been too tough for a sneaky charmer to make friends with the older and drabber Regina. She was a no-longer-young orphan who didn't know a soul up there in the mountains."

Amanda nodded understandingly. Vail said, "I follow your drift so far. But how could even the only friend she had convince the real Regina Masterson to swap places with her?"

Longarm's voice was grim as he replied, "Easy. Etta Bacon murdered her. There'd have been a death certificate on file with Lake County if the real Regina Masterson had died any *other* way and, as you just said, not even a best friend would turn all her property over to you, *willingly*. They'd probably been living together a

177

spell before Etta made her move. Folk on the same mountain had gotten used to two shy spinsters who sort of kept to themselves. When one wasn't there anymore, nobody had cause to worry about it, or to question the simple fact that a gal they'd seen about the property for some time was the proper owner, when she *said* she was."

Amanda repressed a shudder and said, "Brrr! She must have been a really cold-blooded little monster!"

Longarm didn't want to get into how cold Miss Etta had been in bed. He said, "None of the Bacons was nice. But, like I said, she was smarter than the rest. She didn't know how long she could get away with pretending to be the proper owner of the property. So she put it on the market, cheap, hoping to be on her way with a modest profit and nobody the wiser."

He reached for a cheroot of his own as he continued, "Enter Howard Windy Winger, still no more than a sort of uncouth mining man, that far back. As they dickered over the price, both unattached, hard-drinking and horny, nature took its course and the next thing he knew he was hooked. It must have surprised her as well. For, like Gypsies, the Bacons hardly ever married up with outsiders. She may well have decided to marry up with him here in the city to avoid ducking more than rice as they left for their honeymoon. But once she and her dumb rich husband were settled in, with her ruling the roost, her black-sheep kin no doubt forgave her. She was pushy and ambitious. Next thing old Winger knew she had him running for office and they were on their way to Washington."

Amanda frowned thoughtfully and said, "I don't see how you can say she was *smart,* Custis. Once she was married to a man on his way up, why didn't she just drop her disgusting relations?"

Vail said, "I can answer that. I'm older. It ain't easy to just drop bad pennies. Even nicer folk have trouble with 'em turning up. Do you think the James boys would want to lose touch of a kid sister who married up with a rich senator?"

Longarm nodded and said, "She'd been brung up just as crooked by nature. A heap of folk in prison right now wouldn't be there if they had the sense to see that once you got it all you don't need to steal no more. As the pampered darling of a rich old fool she likely spent more on dresses than her kin made robbing. But they was still *kin* and, being in a position to help out, she done what she could."

"That stone quarry!" Vail gasped. "Senator Winger said he'd forgot he owned that property until you and the boys just about ruined it on him!"

Longarm nodded and said, "Before that it was a re-mote cow camp in the Nebraska sand hills. When Winger bought that stone quarry as an investment, no-ticed what a bad investment it was, and put it back on the market, cheap, his wife sort of pigeonholed the papers for him. He had lots more business and political correspondence and she was a big help with such mat-ters to a semi-illiterate. All she had to do was forget to sell it and pay the occasional and mighty modest tax bills she got to open, first, with the rest of their mail. The quarry made a swell hideout, until we blew it up under most of the gang left over from that ill-advised train robbery."

Vail smiled and said, "Well, I never. But hold on, Longarm. We might never have learned about that slick hideout if the Wingers had just left you alone. What call did even a treacherous witch like her have to talk her husband into pestering you, or sending John Henry Cal-

179

houn to gun you behind city hall? Neither one of them gents was Bacons, was they?"

Longarm said, "You're getting ahead of the tale, Billy. Those hired bodyguards were Senator Winger's notion. He probably got to worrying, over the years, about mysterious strangers lurking about or crawfishing back into the shadows just as he was coming home to his dear little woman. The extra help would have cramped her style, had not she somehow subverted them to her own bidding."

Amanda pursed her lips and said primly, "I'll bet I know just how she got those guns her husband hired under her thumb. It must have been just disgusting when her husband was away and they got to play spin the bottle with her!"

Longarm smiled tolerantly and said, "Well, there was plenty of bottles to play with. But let's stick to dirty doings we can be sure about."

He flicked some ash on the rug, ignoring the dirty look Vail shot at him, and said, "The special hearings were the senator's *own* grand notion. She'd no doubt pillow-talked him into opposing the death penalty and convinced him pistol-whipping a suspect was mean, as a favor to her kin, but the last thing she wanted was a trip out west where lots more people knew both the gals she'd been in her time. She was no doubt doing her best to stay out of the public eye as she hoped for the best. Then her kinsman, Big Bob Bacon, got picked up in Stateline. She knew he was dumb, even for a Bacon. She had to get him out of the hands of the law, dead or alive, and she knew her kinsmen were almost as dumb. So she fired two of her bodyguards, official, to give them an excuse for not going back to Washington with her and the other four when she gave her husband any old excuse and headed east aboard that private car."

Vail shook his head and said, "No she never. Calhoun was still on their payroll when he shot it out with you in the alley. That was what made Senator Winger so mad at you to begin with."

Longarm took a drag on his cheroot and growled, "I'm never going to finish an already complicated tale if you keep butting in so nit-picky, boss. Winger was already set to rake me and other local lawmen over the coals. He'd have really had fun with Smiley and Dutch. Remember the time Dutch gunned a suspect down like a dog at Colfax and Broadway, during the rush hour? Winger's woman knew who was slated to appear before that select committee before it ever got out here. Since, in all modesty, she must have known my rep for fighting back, she assumed, correctly, that I'd start trying to dig up all the dirt I could find to fling back at the senator. She was the dirtiest thing he had in his background. They may or may not have guessed I'd be the senior deputy you'd send to pick up an important want like Big Bob. At any rate, she ordered Calhoun to keep an eye on me. So that's what he was doing when I, in all innocence, approached the back door of the Hall of Records, down that alley. He didn't know I was just taking a shortcut to work. He thought I was snooping into the past of Denver's own Regina Masterson. The *real* one. He reacted as the fake Regina had told him to and we all know how that turned out. Senator Winger clouded up and rained all over me for gunning his private gun because, without his wife in town to talk to, he honestly thought I had. I don't know why there was a record of her firing Dove and none on Calhoun. There should have been. Maybe she was just in a hurry."

"Back to Washington?" asked Amanda with a puzzled frown.

Longarm shook his head and said, "Her *car* went

east that far, along with the bodyguards who wouldn't let anyone bother the lady enough to notice she didn't seem to be on it. She got off at Stateline with a bottle of Bombay gin and a lot of money. She bought out the saloon across from the local lockup so she and a couple of her slicker kinsmen could use it as a base of operations. The more professional Cyrus Dove was supposed to lead the others when they busted Big Bob out. She needed more professional help than that. On their way across the prairie the not-as-bright Bacons thought they saw a chance to rob that train and got shot up and scattered for their pains."

Vail grinned wolfishly and chimed in with, "That made you even more famous when you arrived to pick up the prisoner across the way, right?"

Longarm nodded and said, "Considering how wrong things were going for her by then, I got to give her a gold star for effort. The only thing they still had going for them was that jurisdictional dispute. Hoping I was stuck for the moment, she got word to old Cyrus Dove, camped out on the prairie alone, because he was just too sly to engage in unplanned train robberies. He rode in to kill me. When that didn't work either, old Etta stayed as cool as ever, took my side with the town law, and tried to befriend me long enough to come up with some other treachery."

Amanda raised an eyebrow and asked, "Oh? And just how did she go about making friends with you, Custis?"

He met her eyes with an innocent smile and some effort before he said, truthfully enough when one studied on it, "As a matter of fact she did try to get me to spend the night with her. Only I didn't. I busted Big Bob out and, just as she'd feared, I did get a line on that quarry out of him before he got so disgusting I had to bury him in Sand Creek wash. Meanwhile, she'd tried

182

to throw us of by wiring nobody at all in Golden. She was likely worried most about my ever looking for hints of her past down in Leadville. She forgot or didn't know the quarry was in Jefferson County. It still slowed us down and had me scouting for a short male Bacon who she'd impersonated. She surely was a *sneaky* little thing."

Vail protested, "Don't stop now, dang it. Why in thunder did she stage that fool fake kidnapping, later?"

Amanda said, "He's right. That made no sense at all. Had I been that brazen hussy I'd have quit while I was ahead! You'd have never caught her and exposed her grotesque double life if she'd been content to just leave it be and go back to being a fashionable Washington hostess!"

Longarm shook his head and told her, "Some gals just don't think as brazen, I reckon. It's true she was rid of most of her black-sheep kin, thanks to me and the boys. She might well have entertained the notion of going straight at last. It must have been tedious to serve tea to her society pals and keep one ear cocked for gun-play at the same time. But to do that, she had to tidy up. Her husband kept sending wires to Washington, begging her to come back out here and watch him strut his stuff at the opera house. Her confederates were able to relay such wires and her sweet excuses as she went on running that saloon in Stateline. She was running out of sweet excuses, but she didn't dare show herself at those hearings, where any number of other ladies in the audience might have known the *real* Regina. So she decided to kill a mess of birds at the same time. She wired her husband she was on her way back to him. Then she sent for her private car and met it, say, in Kansas City. At least some of her house servants had to be covering up for her. That's Senator's Winger's problem if he ever sobers up. They might have only thought they were covering up a love affair for the lady of the house."

Vail growled, "Get to the more exciting parts."

So Longarm nodded and said, "Somewhere in the night, as the train was no doubt rolling noisy, the sneaky gal convinced one of her four hired guns to help her do the other three in. Then she shot him. He tried to scrawl *double cross* on the rug, but died before he could make more than the first two letters. When the train got to Stateline in the wee small hours, she simply got off and went back to serving beer and bad piano music in an out-of-the-way place where nobody had any reason to take her for a kidnapped lady."

"Until you showed up," said Vail, beaming fondly.

Longarm said, "I wasn't supposed to. I'd finished my original mission to Stateline. All of us were supposed to hunt in circles until her unsettled husband called off the hearings and went on back east. Once the coast was clear, she no doubt meant to do in old Kevin and that last cousin that Dutch shot instead. Then she'd be free to wash the tea or whatever out of her hair, go on back to her husband, and tell him she'd escaped from her mean captors, still pure. Some men will believe anything."

Amanda must have agreed with him about that. She said, "My God, it would have worked, if *you* hadn't known so much about women. What put you on to her sneaky double life, Custis?"

He shrugged and said, "It was just too double, I reckon. The few folk I could find who remembered the shy Regina Masterson kept recalling her as no fun at all. Yet everyone who'd met her as Windy Winger's woman described her as lively, good-looking, and mighty well preserved for a forty-year-old gal who drank so regular. I know kids can change, growing up. But it did strike me odd that a gal who'd still been a shy spinster at the age of thirty could have blossomed *that* much. If anything, her getting stuck with a crude windbag like old Winger should have slowed her down a mite. But to tell the pure truth, I was only guessing 'til I confronted her earlier today and she and her kin commenced to prove my point."

Vail fished out his pocket watch, consulted it gravely, and said, "My own old woman is going to shoot me if I don't get home for supper soon. You done good and I'm proud of you, Longarm. I left Senator Winger a broken man. Even if he gets elected again this fall, I doubt he'll ever pester us no more." Then he got to his feet and left Longarm and Amanda Bleeker to sort out their own plans for the evening. She smiled across the table at him wistfully to say, "Well, if there's to be no hearings after all, I guess I've done all I can for you, eh?"

He took her hand again to say, "Honey, you ain't even started. But I reckon I'd better take you out for some chili, first."

Watch for

LONGARM AND THE LONE STAR FRAME

eighth *Longarm Giant Novel*

and

**LONGARM AND THE NEW MEXICO
SHOOT-OUT**

one hundred eighteenth novel in the bold
LONGARM series from Jove

Both coming in October!